Also by Jean Ure

Secret Meeting
Passion Flower
Pumpkin Pie
Shrinking Violet
Boys on the Brain
Skinny Melon and Me
Becky Bananas, This is Your Life!
Fruit and Nutcase
The Secret Life of Sally Tomato*
Family Fan Club
Collins Book of Ballet and Dance Stories (ed.)

and for younger readers

Dazzling Danny
Daisy May
Monster in the Mirror

Also available on tape, read by John Pickard

Is Anybody There?

JEAN URE

Illustrated by Karen Donnelly

HarperCollins *Children's Books*

For Emily Crye

This edition produced for The Book People Ltd,
Hall Wood Avenue, Haydock, St Helens, WA11 9UL

First published in Great Britain by HarperCollins *Children's Books* 2004
HarperCollins *Children's Books* is a division of HarperCollins*Publishers* Ltd,
77-85 Fulham Palace Road, Hammersmith,
London W6 8JB

The HarperCollins *Children's Books* website address is
www.harpercollinschildrensbooks.co.uk

1 3 5 7 9 8 6 4 2

Text © Jean Ure 2004
Illustrations © Karen Donnelly 2004

ISBN 978 0 00 781601 9

The author and illustrator assert the moral right to be
identified as the author and illustrator of the work.

Printed and bound in India by
Thomson Press (India) Ltd.

one

LAST CHRISTMAS WHEN I was in Year 8, I did this really dumb thing. The dumbest thing I have ever done in all my life. *I got into a car with someone I didn't know.*

OK, so I was only just turned thirteen, which in my experience is an age when you tend to act a bit stupid, thinking to yourself that you are now practically grown up and don't need to obey your mum's silly little niggly rules any more. Also, I have to say, it wasn't like I'd never met the guy. I mean, I knew his name, I knew who he was. I even knew where he lived. But I'd only met him just the one time, just to say hello to, and even that was enough to tell me that he was a bit – well, different. Definitely not the same as other people. In any case, thirteen is *way* old enough to know better. We're all taught back in Reception that you don't go off with strangers.

"And that," as Mum was always drumming into me, "means the man next door, the man over the road, the butcher, the baker, the candlestick maker... you don't go with *anyone*. Got it?" And out loud I would say, "Yes, Mum!" while inside I would be thinking, "This is just *so* too much."

Mind you, Dad is every bit as bad, in fact I'm not sure he's not even worse. Whenever I go up to Birmingham, to stay with him and his new wife Irene, it's, "Where do you want to go? We'll take you! You can't go on your own. Not in Birmingham." Like Birmingham is one big bad place full of child molesters. Dad says it's not that, it's just that Birmingham is a city, and I am not used to being in a city.

"I'm sure at home your mother lets you go wherever you want."

I wish! Though actually, to be honest, after last Christmas, I didn't want to go anywhere on my own. It took me ages to get my confidence back.

*

How it all started, really, was one wet Saturday afternoon towards the end of term; the Christmas term. Chloe and Dee had come round, and we were up in my bedroom. We were huge best mates in those days, the three of us. We'd all gone to St Mary Day from different schools, but we'd palled up immediately. We spent most Saturdays either round at my house, or Dee's; just occasionally we'd go to Chloe's, but Chloe had to share a bedroom with her little sister, who was one big pain and totally hyperactive, if you ask me. So we didn't go there often as it led to *scenes*, with Jade and Chloe threatening to punch each other's teeth down their

throats or pull their hair out by the roots. Come to think of it, Chloe herself is a bit hyperactive. She's always on the move, can't sit still, can't keep quiet. Can't stop *giggling* (when she's not fighting with her sister). It gets her into terrible trouble at school.

Dee, on the other hand, is quite cool and laid back. She is a very serious sort of person. I suppose I would have to say that I am midway between the two. Sometimes I have fits of the giggles, other times I contemplate life and what it all means,

and try to think deeply about God and religion and stuff. But I can see, now, looking back on it, that we were a fairly odd sort of threesome. However, we did have a lot of fun, before I went and ruined it all.

That particular Saturday afternoon, that Saturday at the end of term, it was pouring with rain drip drip dripping off the trees, plink plonk into the water butt. We were upstairs in my room, all cosily huddled under my duvet with Dee and Chloe doing their best to push me into playing The Game – which makes me think that really, I suppose, before going any further, I should stop and explain what the Game is all about.

OK. Basically it's about me being a bit psychic. Well, more than a bit, actually. According to Mum, I have "the gift". Mum is also psychic; I get it from her. Only she says that with me it is even stronger than it is with her, or will be, when I am grown up. Mum makes her living as a professional clairvoyant. People come to visit her, and she does

Not my mum!

readings for them. It is all quite honest and above board. Mum is *not* a charlatan! She explained to me, once, how clairvoyant simply means "seeing clearly". She doesn't pretend to be able to tell what is going to happen in the future. She can tell what *might* happen, if people keep on

9

doing the things that they are doing, but it is up to them whether they act on what she says. She is not here to change people's lives for them; only they can do that. She doesn't use tarot cards or a ouija board, she doesn't use a crystal ball, or call up spirits from the other side.

What Mum does, she asks people to give her some object that they have handled, like it might be a watch, or a bracelet, just something small and personal, and by holding it, and concentrating, she can, like, see inside a person's mind. She can tell them things about themselves that they hadn't realised they knew; things that are hidden deep within them. Things, sometimes, that they have deliberately suppressed.

Or maybe she'll dredge up something from their past that they'd forgotten, and suddenly everything will fall into place and make sense and they'll say, "Ah! Yes. *Now* I understand."

Some people just come to her out of curiosity; others come because they are unhappy or in trouble. It is very satisfying, Mum says, when you can help someone, but it is also very draining. It takes ever such a lot out of her, which is why she tries not to do more than three sessions in a day. Unfortunately, these sessions quite often take place in the evening or at weekends, which is a bit of a drag, but I have grown used to it. I don't think Dad ever did, only with him it wasn't just people coming round and spoiling his evenings, it was the whole thing about Mum being psychic. He just couldn't handle it, is what Mum says.

"He found it a bit creepy; it really used to upset him, poor man! But if you've got it, you've got it. It's not something you can just ignore."

It was quite by chance that we discovered I had it. I mean, Mum didn't give me tests, or anything like that. It happened unexpectedly, without any warning, when I was nine years old. My nan had just died, and Mum was very sad about it, and so was I, although Nan had been ill for a long time and I had never really known her any other way. I'd gone over to the nursing home with Mum, to collect Nan's stuff, and when we brought it back Mum said that I could have Nan's gold propelling pencil to keep, in memory of her.

"Nan loved that pencil! Grandad gave it to her, when they were first married. She'd have liked you to have it."

I don't think I'd ever handled a propelling pencil before. While Mum was in the kitchen making tea, I sat playing with it, twiddling the top and making the lead go up and down, and all of a sudden this great surge of joy came over me; I laughed and jumped up, and started dancing all around the room. Mum came in in the middle of it.

"Well, I'm glad to see one of us is happy," she said. There was just this tiny note of reproach in her voice, and it made me feel guilty because how could I be laughing and dancing when Nan had just died? I said to Mum, "I don't really feel happy. It was Nan! She's the one that was happy."

"How do you mean?" said Mum.

"She was with someone – a man – and they were laughing. And then she kissed him, and they started dancing. And she was just so happy!"

"Jo," said Mum, "what are you talking about?"

"Nan!" I held out the pencil. "I saw her! When she was young." And then I stopped, because obviously I hadn't even been born when Nan was young, so how could I possibly have known that it was her? But I had!

Mum questioned me closely. She made me look at pictures, and I found the man that Nan had been dancing with. It was my grandad, who I'd never met. Doubtfully, Mum said, "Of course, you've seen photographs of him. But all the same..."

Mum was really upset, and I couldn't understand it. "Mum, she was happy!" I cried. "Nan was happy!"

I thought it would make Mum happy, knowing that, but it didn't seem to. She said, "Oh, this cursed legacy!" I said, "Who's Kirsty Leggaty?" Well, I mean, I was only nine; what did I know? Mum then told me that I had the gift. She said she'd been hoping and praying that I wouldn't have, because although it could be a power for good it didn't make for an easy life.

I said, "But it was nice, seeing Nan!"

I think my face must have crumpled, because Mum hugged me and said, "Oh, darling, I'm sure it was. May all your visions be as happy!"

We didn't talk any more about it for a while after that. I didn't have any more visions, either; not that I can remember. Just one or two when I was in Year 6, but nothing to worry about. Nothing upsetting. It got a bit annoying when I changed schools and it started happening more regularly, but I very soon learnt how to recognise the signs and take avoiding action. Nowadays, I can almost always blot it out. You have to blot things out, or life would become intolerable. Mum is lucky that way, she doesn't have to. This is why she says my gift is more powerful than hers. Mum actually needs someone to be there, in person, before anything can get through. On the other hand she has to concentrate far harder than I do, which is why it tends to wear her out.

On my eleventh birthday, Mum told me that I was old enough, now, to take responsibility for the gift I had been given.

"I nearly said, 'saddled with', but that wouldn't be fair. You can do so much good with it, Jo! But you must treat it with respect. It's not something to just play around with. It's not a toy."

She told me that just as I could do good with it, I could also do harm.

"Do you understand me? I hope you do, because this is serious."

I *said* that I understood, but I don't really think I did. It was hard to see what harm it could do, just amusing my friends now and again. Anyway I didn't ever boast about being clairvoyant, but when Chloe and Dee asked me one day what my mum did, and I told them, and they wanted to know whether I could do it, too – well, naturally, I said yes. So then they wanted me to show them, which I knew Mum would have said I shouldn't; I knew she would have said it was treating my gift like a toy. But I just didn't see what was so wrong about it!

"It's only a bit of *fun*."

That was Chloe. Everything is a bit of fun with Chloe. If things aren't fun, she can't see any point in doing them. An attitude which does not go down too well with some of our teachers! Dee, being more serious, said that she could "sort of understand" why Mum was concerned.

"After all, being clairvoyant isn't exactly the same as being musical, or being able to dance, or... do gymnastics, or something."

"Whoever said it was?" wondered Chloe.

"What I *mean*," said Dee, "is you're not going to hurt anyone, just playing the piano. But you might hurt

someone getting into their mind. Specially if they didn't want you to, or you discovered something scary."

"Like what?" said Chloe.

"Like if someone was going to die." said Dee. At which Chloe gave a delighted screech and clutched herself round the middle. Honestly! She is just *so* ghoulish. She is totally mad about horror films, or anything with blood. Not me! *Urgh.*

"That would be so gross!" squealed Chloe.

I said, "Yes, it would. How would you like it if I saw that *you* were going to die?"

17

That shut her up. Well, for a little bit. But there and then, we laid down rules. *If* we were going to play the Game, we were only going to do it using objects that belonged to people who'd given their permission.

"Otherwise," I said, "it'd be like...well, like prying into someone's private affairs."

Dee agreed immediately, and after a bit so did Chloe. She said she thought it was a pity, as she would have liked me to do some of the teachers, she thought that would be fun, but Dee and I made her promise – "On your honour!" – that she wouldn't ever cheat. That way, we thought it would be safe.

Even so, we didn't play The Game too often. For one thing, I had to be in the mood, and for another I always had this slight guilt feeling, like maybe I was doing what Mum had warned me not to: using my gift "irresponsibly". It did niggle at me every now and again, but I told myself that it was just Mum, fussing. Mums do fuss! All the time, over just about everything. You have to decide for yourself whether it's a justified fuss, or just a Mum fuss. If it's just a Mum fuss, then it's OK to ignore it. Well, anyway, that's what I told myself.

That particular Saturday, what with it being nearly the end of term and Christmas only a couple of weeks away,

I guess it was a bit like, "So what? Just a Mum fuss!" We messed about for a while, and I did Chloe's cousin Dulcie, and had Chloe in fits of the giggles when I saw "Seven little people... I am definitely seeing seven little people! I can't work out what it means."

Dee said, "Maybe she's going to get married and have seven babies." and Chloe squealed and rolled herself up in the duvet.

"Is she happy about it?" said Dee.

"Mm... yes. I think so. But she's kind of a bit... anxious."

"You would be," said Dee, "if you were going to have seven babies!"

Chloe squealed again and shot out of the duvet. "She's not going to have seven babies! She's playing Snow White in her end-of-term play... *Snow White and the Seven Dwarfs*!"

"That is *so* politically incorrect," said Dee.

"It's better than having seven babies," said Chloe. "Let's do another one! Do my Auntie Podge. Look! This is her hanky. I did ask her."

But I didn't want to do Chloe's Auntie Podge. "I'm tired," I said. "I've had enough."

"But I promised!" wailed Chloe. "I said you'd do her!"

"I'll do her another day."

For a minute it looked like Chloe was going to go off into one of her sulks, but then she suddenly snatched my nightie from under the pillow and cried, "OK, I'll do you! I'll tell you what *you're* thinking..." She scrunched the nightie into a ball and made this big production of screwing her eyes tight shut and swaying to and fro (which I do *not* do, though I do close my eyes). After almost swaying herself dizzy, she began to chant in this silly, spooky voice.

"Is anybody the-e-e-re? Is anybody the-e-e-re? I see something! I see... a shape! I see... a boy! I see... *DANNY HARVEY*!"

I immediately turned bright pillar-box red.

"Told you so, told you so!" Triumphantly, Chloe hurled my scrunched up nightie at Dee. "Told you she was mad about him!"

"I am not," I snapped; but by now my face was practically in flames, so fat chance of anyone believing me. The truth was, I'd had a thing about Danny Harvey ever since half term, when he'd come to our Fête Day with his mum and dad. (His sister Claire's in Year 7.)

He'd visited the cuddly toy stall that I was helping look after. He'd bought a pink bunny rabbit! From *me*. I thought it was so cool, a Year 10 boy buying a bunny rabbit. I may not know as much as I

would like to
about boys, but even I know that
they would mostly be too embarrassed to buy a cuddly toy!

Mary Day, unfortunately, is an all-girls' school, so we don't get much of a chance to mix with boys; and if, like me, you are an only child, and specially if your mum and dad have split up, you practically live the life of a nun. Like, the opposite sex is utterly mysterious and you might just as well hope to meet aliens from outer space as an actual *boy*. But I knew where Danny went to school, it was Cromwell House, just down the road from Mary's, so by

using a different bus stop, and doing a bit of carefully timed lingering and lurking, I did occasionally manage to catch a glimpse of him. For weeks and weeks a glimpse was all, but just a few days ago, joy and bliss! He'd smiled at me and said "Hi". He'd remembered! He'd recognised me! He knew I was the one that had sold him the bunny! Which, needless to say, had set me off all over again. Just as I thought I might be getting over it...

"Poor you," said Dee; and I sighed, and she hugged me. And although she didn't say it, I knew what she was thinking: *Poor old Jo! She doesn't stand a chance.*

It was then that Chloe had her bright idea. We knew that Danny worked weekends and Thursday evenings at the Pizza Palace in the High Street (I had my spies!), so why didn't we organise an end-of-term celebration for the day we broke up, which just happened to be a Thursday?

"We could say it's for everyone in our class, 'cos they won't all come, but if it's just the three of us it might look kind of obvious, or *parents* might even want to be there..."

Dee and I groaned.

"Whereas if it's for the whole class," said Chloe, "they're more likely to let us go by ourselves. And *then*" – she beamed at me – "you can get all dressed up and flirt as much as you like!"

Naturally I denied that I would do any such thing; but already I was mentally whizzing through my wardrobe wondering what to wear...

two

FIFTEEN OF US signed up for our end-of-term celebration. We arranged to meet at the Pizza Place at six o'clock so that we could be home by nine, which was what most people's parents laid down as the deadline, it being December, and dark, and the High Street being full of pubs and clubs and wine bars, not to mention Unsavoury Types that hung about in shop doorways. It was Mum who said they were unsavoury.

"Why do you have to go into town? Why can't you find somewhere local?"

I said, "Because not everybody lives somewhere local." Plus anywhere local is totally naff. "Anyway," I said, "you don't have to worry... Dee's dad will come and pick us up."

"So long as he does," said Mum.

I said, "Mum, he *will*."

Dee lives just a bit further out from Tanfield, which is the boring suburb where I am doomed to dwell; her dad always gives me a lift. So Mum said all right, in that case she would let me go, and I rushed off to ransack my wardrobe and see what I had that was even remotely wearable, and to ring Dee and tell her that she could go ahead and book a table, or get her mum to.

Of the three of us, it was always Dee who did the organising. Chloe was too scatty, she would be bound to get the wrong day, or the wrong time; even wrong *year*. Mum used to say she was "mercurial". Dee and I just said she was useless. I am not useless, but Dee is one of those people who always has everything under control. She's the same at school. She always knows what's been set for homework, she's always *done* her homework. She's the one who's always filled in her timetable correctly, the one who tells the rest of us where we're meant to be, and when. I bet you anything you like she'll end up as head girl, keeping us all in order.

But, oh dear, it was so sad! So *unfair*. The day before our celebration poor old Dee was carted off to hospital with an asthma attack. She has asthma really badly; her mum said she would never be fit enough by Thursday evening.

I was really upset for her, especially after all the hard work she'd put in, but also it meant I had to tell Mum that Mr Franklin wouldn't be picking me up any more.

He probably would have done, if I'd asked him, but Mum wouldn't hear of it. She said, "We can't impose on people like that!" But Mum herself couldn't come and fetch me, she had two sessions booked for that evening, and she said she certainly wasn't letting me make my own way back.

"Not at that time of night. Not in this town. No way!"

She told me I was to ring Albert and get myself a cab. Albert is one of her regulars, he's been coming to her for years. He also happens to run a minicab service, which comes in useful as Mum says he can be relied upon. She wouldn't normally let me go anywhere near a minicab, but Albert is like a mother hen. When I was little he quite often used to pick me up after school, and always got most tremendously fussed if I wasn't waiting exactly where I had been told to wait.

"A lot of bad people around! You can't be too careful."

I couldn't help feeling that a cab all the way from the High Street out to Tanfield was a bit of an extravagance when there was a perfectly good bus that would take me practically door to door, but I didn't say anything as I knew Mum would freak if I even so much as hinted at jumping on a bus. Instead, I concentrated all my energies on what I was going to wear.

It is so important, deciding what you are going to wear! There are different clothes for different occasions, and if you don't get it right you can find that you have turned up in jeans and trainers while everyone else is dressed to kill. Or even worse, *you* are dressed to kill and everyone else is in jeans and trainers. That is truly squirm-making!

Actually, however, since the contents of my wardrobe would probably fit quite comfortably into a couple of carrier bags, I didn't really have much choice. I only seem to have clothes for two occasions, one of them being school and the other being – everything else!

Which is OK as I am not really a dressing-up sort of person, being tallish and skinnyish without actually having any figure; not to speak of. No bum, no boobs. Just straight up and down. What can you do?

I used to envy the others so much! They might not be drop dead gorgeous, but even Dee, who is so slim and bendy, has some shape. She also has silvery blonde hair, cut very smooth and shiny, and always looks just so so neat. Chloe is just the opposite. She is very small and chunky and has no dress sense whatsoever, but because of being vivacious manages to look really bright and perky, like a little animated pixie. I probably look more like a sort of... stick arrangement. Mum says that I will "grow into myself". Meaning, I think, that I will be OK when I finally manage to achieve something resembling a figure.

30

Meanwhile, as I await that glorious day, I tend to wear... you've got it! Jeans and trainers. Which is what I put on for the celebration. Dee once told me that I looked good in jeans as I have these very long legs, like I'm walking on stilts. They are, however, not particularly inspiring – the jeans, that is. So to go with them I found a sparkly top, pale pink, that I'd hardly ever worn. I did my hair into a plait, one of those that's tight into your head rather than a pigtail. I think pigtails are a bit childish, all thumping about, but Dee said that having my hair pulled back made me look sophisticated. To top it off, I wore this very chic hat that I found in a charity shop. It's like a man's hat, I think it's called a fedora. It's got a high crown and a small brim, and is made from soft felt. It looks really great with jeans!

I was quite pleased when I studied myself in the mirror. The only thing wrong was the trainers. What I would really like to have had, what I had been positively lusting after ever since I'd seen them in a shoe shop  in town, was a pair of glitter boots. You could get them in either silver with red tassels, or gold with green. It was the silver ones I was lusting after! I'd shown them to Mum, who *predictably* had said they were totally impractical and wouldn't last five minutes. But five minutes was all I needed! I was busy saving up, and was praying they would still be there when I'd reached my goal. Saving money, though, is *so* difficult. I kept finding other things that I just desperately had to have! Entire continents could come and go by the time I managed to get fifty pounds in my account.

So I wore my tatty old trainers and my tatty old denim jacket, and Mum got the car out and drove me into town. As she dropped me off outside the Pizza Palace she said, "Shall I ring Albert and book a cab for you?" I was horrified. I said, "Mum, no! I can do it." The last thing I wanted was Albert turning up, all mother hennish, and dragging me off before we'd properly finished. It's horrid if you're the first one to leave. You imagine all the others staying on to have fun after you've gone.

Mum said, "Well, all right, have it your way – but I want you back no later than nine o'clock. You'd better ring for a cab at 8.30, just to be on the safe side. And don't you pull that face at me, my girl! You may think you're some kind of big shot, being in Year 8, but you're still only th—"

"Yeah, yeah!" I hopped out of the car and slammed the door shut behind me. I'd just seen Mel Sanders go mincing into the restaurant, all got up like a Christmas tree.

What was more, *she was wearing my boots*. I could see the little tassels swinging as she walked. Fortunately she'd gone for the gold ones, not the silver; all the same, it was a bad moment.

"Joanne?" Mum was banging on the window at me, pointing at her watch. I flapped a hand.

"It's all right, I heard you. *Don't fuss!*"

Of the fifteen of us, only ten actually turned up, but ten was probably about right, given the amount of noise we made! To be honest, I didn't actually realise we were making any until a woman at a table nearby came over and asked if we could "be a little bit quieter... I can hardly hear myself think!"

So then I stopped to listen, and I had to admit, she had a point. I have noticed that adults are very sensitive to decibel levels, and ours was certainly well up. Chloe, sitting next to me, was screeching at the top of her voice, which is quite loud enough even when she isn't screeching. Louise Patterson, at the far end of the table, was doing her best to stuff half her pizza into someone's mouth, Carrie Newman was having hysterics (well, that's what it sounded like), Lee Williams seemed to have got drunk on Coca Cola and Marsha Tate was tipping backwards on her chair, and honking like a car horn.

Our mums would *not* have been pleased. Nor would our class teacher, Mrs Monahan. She was always on about "gracious behaviour in public". We weren't behaving very graciously! But most of us hadn't ever been out for a meal on our own before, i.e. without grown-ups to keep us in their vice-like grip. I know I hadn't. I suppose it rather went to our heads, but it was the best fun.

I have to say, however, that it would have been even huger fun if Mel Sanders hadn't been there. That girl is so... obnoxious! She is so *obvious*. Where members of the opposite sex are concerned, I mean. She is one of those people, she only has to catch the merest glimpse of a boy in the far dim distance and she goes completely hyper. If there is one actually sharing her breathing space, well, wow! That is *it*. Fizz, bang, wallop, firing on all cylinders. Eyes flashing, teeth gleaming, boobs thrust

out as far as they will go. (Which isn't very far, as a matter of fact, but she makes it look as if it is.) I guess it's something to do with her hormones, she probably has too many of them, and she just can't help herself. For all I know, it could even be some kind of disease. All I can say is that the effect is extremely irritating since boys, poor things, seem incapable of taking their eyes off her. It's like she has some kind of mesmeric power.

In this case it was specially irritating as clever Chloe had managed to get us moved from the first table they gave us, where a *girl* came to take our order, to another one over by the window. She had been watching, with her beady eyes, and had seen that over by the window was where Dreamboy Danny operated. I hasten to add that *I* didn't call him Dreamboy. I have better taste than that! Dreamboy was Chloe's nickname for him.

"He's over there," she whispered. "Let's move!"

She claimed she was too near the smoking area ("I get this *really* bad asthma") so we all trooped over to the windows and there was Danny, with his order pad – and there was Mel, with her eyes going into overdrive, and I might just as well not have been there. If it *is* a disease that she's got, I wouldn't mind having a bit of it myself. Not enough to make me ill, or anything; but it would be nice to be able to mesmerise boys. As it was, I don't think Danny even noticed me; or if he did, he didn't show any signs of actual recognition. I guess maybe I look different when I'm not in school uniform. All the same... big sigh! He'd recognise Mel if she turned up in a bin bag.

Round about half past eight, people's parents started arriving and I dutifully rang Albert on my mobile, only I couldn't get through as the number was engaged, and while I was waiting for it to become unengaged I started thinking things to myself. It was totally stupid spending all that money on a cab when I could just as easily walk a few hundred yards up the road and catch a bus. I'd still be home by nine – well, nine*ish* – and I wouldn't need to tell Mum how I'd got there. Which meant I could put the money I'd saved towards the glitter boots! I wanted those boots more than ever after seeing Mel in a pair. I think I felt that if I had the boots I might also have the hypnosis thing and be able to get boys to take notice of me. Maybe. I know it was bad, when I'd given Mum my word, but I was, like, desperate. I'd just spent the whole evening being totally overlooked by the boy I loved! Well, OK, perhaps love is a bit strong, but I truly did fancy him like crazy.

Believe me, if you have never experienced it, I am here to tell you that fancying a boy who has eyes Only for Another can make you behave in ways you normally wouldn't dream of. At any rate, that is my excuse because it is the only one I can think of.

I snatched up my jacket and rushed out into the night. I wasn't bothered about being one of the first to leave; I just wanted to add Mum's cab money to my boot fund! Unfortunately, owing to the stupid one-way system, you can't actually catch a bus to Tanfield directly outside the Pizza Palace but have to go trailing round the side roads, which at that time of night are more or less deserted.

I am not at all a nervous kind of person. I really don't mind being out on my own in the dark – not that I am ever allowed to be – but I must admit, it was a bit scary, waiting for the bus at an empty bus stop in this great concrete canyon, nothing but slab-sided office blocks rising up on either side, and gaping dark holes leading into the bowels of underground car parks. Plus this really spooky orange lighting, and not a single human being to be seen.

I was just beginning to think that maybe I had better go back to the restaurant and ring Albert after all, when a little blue Ka pulled up and the driver wound down the window and called out to me.

"Joanne? It is Joanne, isn't it?"

I'd been all prepared to turn and run. You'd better believe it! But when he called my name, I hesitated.

"Joanne? It's Paul – Dee's brother. Can I give you a lift?"

Well! I relaxed when he said he was Dee's brother. I'd only met him once, a few weeks back, when mostly all we'd said was "Hi"; but obviously, being Dee's brother, he had to be all right. So I said that I would love a lift, and I hopped into the car as quick as could be, feeling mightily pleased with myself. I'd be home well before nine, and could keep *all* of the cab money!

Cosily, as we drove, I prattled on about my boot fund, and our end-of-term celebration, and how Dee had done all the organising and how rotten it was that she hadn't been able to come. I asked Paul how she was, and he said that she was much better and was out of hospital, and then for a while we talked about Dee and her asthma, and how it stopped her doing some of the things she would really have  liked to do, such as horse riding (because of being allergic to horses) and playing hockey (to which I went "Yuck!" as I am forced to play hockey and would far rather not), but I have to say it was quite hard work as I was the one that had to do most of the talking. Fortunately I am not at all shy, but on the other hand I am not a natural chatterer like Chloe, and after a bit I began to run out of things to talk about.

Paul didn't seem bothered, he just smiled and nodded. He did a lot of smiling, but practically no talking at all. I think it is so weird, when people don't communicate. Even if I asked him a question, he mostly only grunted. Or smiled. *Not* very helpful. You do expect some kind of feedback when you're making all that effort. If it hadn't been for me we would have sat there in total silence. But it shouldn't have been up to me! He was the adult. I couldn't remember how old Dee had said he was, or even *if* she had said, but I knew he was her half brother and was loads older than we were. He must have been at least in his twenties. Mid-twenties, at that. I was only just a teenager, for goodness' sake! Why should I have to carry the burden? It wasn't fair, leaving it all to me.

I looked out of the window in a kind of desperation, wondering where we were, and if we were nearly home, and discovered, to my horror, that we were nowhere near home. Spiders' legs of fright went whispering down my spine. We were on totally the wrong road! Instead of taking the  left fork out of town, through Crossley and Benbridge, he'd gone and swung off to the right, down Gravelpit Hill. I'd been too preoccupied racking my brain for things to say to notice.

"Why—" my voice came out in a strangulated squawk. I had to swallow, and start again. "Why are we driving down G-Gravelpit Hill?"

He turned, to look at me. "Didn't Dee say you lived in Tanfield?"

"Y-yes." I swallowed again. "But th-this isn't the way to get there!"

"It does get there," he said. "I promise you! I know where I'm going." He had this very quiet, husky voice, without much expression. It was more frightening than if he'd shouted. "I realise it adds a bit to the journey, but—"

It didn't just add a *bit*, it took us miles out of our way. It took us through open countryside. Fields, and woods, and isolation. And, in the end, it took us to the gravel pits...

"I always come by this route," he said. "I prefer it to the other."

"But it's such a w-waste of p-petrol!" I said.

"Well – yes." He smiled. "I suppose it is; I never thought of it like that. But it's so much nicer than the main road. Don't you think?"

I couldn't answer him; my mouth had gone dry. I suddenly sensed that I was in terrible danger. I had made the most stupid mistake... I should never have got into the car! And oh, it is true, it is absolutely true, what they say, that at moments like that your blood just seems to turn to water, the bottom of your stomach feels like it has dropped out, and you get cold and shaky and a kind of dread comes over you. The one thing I knew, I had to keep calm. I mustn't panic! If he sussed that I was frightened, it would give him power over me. So long as I just kept my head, I might be able to find a way out.

Doing my best to keep my voice from quavering, I told him that if I didn't get back by nine, Mum would start to worry. "She'll be going frantic!"

In this soft voice, with just a

45

touch of reproach, he said, "Joanne, I really don't think you'd have got home by nine if you'd waited for the bus."

No, but at least I *would* have got home.

"I promised her," I said, "I gave her my word! She'll be worried sick! I think I'd better ring her, and—"

"Yes," he said, "do that."

I scrabbled frantically in my bag, for my mobile. Where was it? *Where was my mobile?* It wasn't there! My mobile wasn't there! I must have left it in the restaurant. In my rush to get away, and catch a bus, and save a few measly pounds, I'd gone and left my mobile in the Pizza Palace. I'd put my entire life in jeopardy for a pair of stupid boots!

Paul said, "What's the matter?"

"My phone," I said. "I've left it behind. I've got to ring Mum, I'll have to go back!"

"There might be one in the glove compartment," he said. He leaned across me to open it and, oh God, I thought my last hour had come! There was a screwdriver in there... one of those really long ones.

I saw his hand close over it, and I immediately lunged sideways in my seat, which threw him off balance so that he jerked at the wheel and the car did this great kangaroo leap. I screamed, and he said, "Sorry! Sorry!" and pulled us back again. "Phew! That was a close shave. Sorry about that. You OK?" He glanced at me as he shut the glove compartment. "It doesn't look as if I've got my phone with me, I'm afraid. But don't worry!" He smiled. "We'll be back in no time. At least coming this way the roads are clear."

I didn't want them to be clear! I wanted them full of traffic, and hold-ups. *I had to get out of that car.*

"You must admit," he said, "it's one of the advantages. And just look at the countryside!" He gestured out of the window, at the dark shapes of pine trees, and the woods looming behind. "I love it out here. You can drive for hours without seeing anyone. It's hard to believe the town's just a couple of miles away."

I knew why he was starting to talk: it was to make me think that everything was normal. But everything wasn't normal!

In a small, tight voice, I said, "I really do need to ring my mum. If I don't ring her she'll wonder where I am. She'll get really worried if she doesn't hear from me. She'll do something stupid, like call the police. I really do think I ought to go back and get my phone!"

"And I really think," he said, firmly, "that it would be better to get you home first and set your mum's mind at rest. We'll be there in a few minutes."

"But I want my phone!" I could hear my voice coming out in this panic-stricken wail. "I need it!"

"You can always call the restaurant when you get in. I'm sure they'll keep it for you. I'll even drive back into town and pick it up for you, if you like. But let's just get you home first. We don't want your mum being worried."

"Please!" I said. I was begging him, now. "I need to go back! I want my phone!"

"Joanne," he said, "mobile phones are not that important. Your mum's peace of mind is at stake here. But OK. OK! If that's what you want, I'll take you back."

I wanted to believe him. I did so want to believe him! But I knew he was only saying it to keep me quiet. If he had really been going to take me back, he would have slowed the car and turned round. Instead, he continued straight on, barrelling down the hill towards the gravel pits. It was the most terrifying moment of my whole life. You just can't believe, until you find yourself in it, that you could ever get yourself in such a situation. This was something that happened to other people! It couldn't be happening to me!

The thing that saved me was the traffic lights. The lights at the intersection with the main Benbridge Road. They were on red, and he was forced to stop. I was out of that car so fast I almost fell over. Coming towards us,

up the hill, heading back into town, was a bus. I regained my balance and hared across the road towards it. I got to the stop just in time... another second and I would have been too late.

I heard him calling after me, "Joanne! I'd have taken you! I was going to go round the roundabout!"

But the roundabout was at the bottom of the hill, where the gravelpits were. I somehow didn't think, if we'd gone that far, that I would ever have come back...

three

IT WAS TWENTY past nine when I finally arrived home. I rang Mum from the cab to tell her that I was on my way; I said I'd had trouble getting through to Albert, and that when I had finally got through, he didn't have a spare cab (keeping fingers firmly crossed that he and Mum would never talk together about it). Mum said rather sharply that that was no excuse, I obviously hadn't rung him early enough.

"I knew you couldn't be trusted! I knew I should have booked in advance."

Then she added that she didn't have time to tell me off right now.

"Miss Allardyce has just called round, she's in one of her states. I've got to go, I shall speak to you later."

By which time, with any luck, she would be too tired to make the effort. Three cheers for Miss Allardyce! Though I have to say that I have never understood how Mum puts up with her. When I was little I used to call her the Handkerchief Lady, because she was always turning up on the doorstep in floods of tears with a handkerchief pressed to her face. In my view she is a total pain, and personally I couldn't be bothered with her, but Mum seems to have masses of patience. She says that she is "a fragile personality", and this, apparently, excuses everything.

Anyway, for once I blessed her – the Handkerchief Lady, that is. I hadn't been looking forward to getting home and having Mum lay into me. I was still feeling quite shaky after my narrow escape. When I'd got back to the Pizza Palace all the others had left but luckily someone had actually picked up my mobile and handed it in, which was not only a major relief ('cos I'd already lost two of them) but also somewhat amazing, since all you ever hear about is mobile phones being stolen. But then I rang Albert, and my hand was so trembly and quaking that I had to have three goes at putting the number in. Even when at last I managed to get through I was terrified that my voice would give me away, because

that was all trembly and quaking, as well. The last thing I wanted was for Albert to start doing his mother hen act.

"What's wrong, poppet? Tell your Uncle Albert! 'fess up... something's happened."

Albert is a darling man and I love him to bits, and so does Mum, but I desperately, desperately didn't want Mum finding out what I'd done. Partly this was because I felt so stupid, and embarrassed, and ashamed;

and partly, of course, because I felt guilty. Not to mention the fact that Mum would never let me out of her sight again.

When I got in, the door of her consulting room was closed, so I guessed that she was with the Handkerchief Lady. Dear, sweet, Handkerchief Lady! If Mum gave her a full hour, it meant I could be safely tucked up in bed before she was through.

While I was getting undressed, my mobile rang. It was Chloe, eager to chat about the night.

"What did you think? Did you enjoy it? I thought it was great! I think we ought to do it again. Only in future," said Chloe, "we'll just ask a *few* people."

I said, "Yes, and Mel Sanders won't be one of them."

Chloe agreed that Mel Sanders would definitely not be one of them. "That girl is just *so* disgusting. She was even making eyes at the old guy behind the bar!"

"He was encouraging her," I said. "They always encourage her. All of them! It's like she has this spell that she casts."

"There isn't anything *magic* about it," said Chloe. "Anyone could do it if they wanted. It's just that some of us happen to have a bit better taste."

"Oh," I said. "Is that what it is?"

"Well, what did you think it was?" said Chloe.

Glumly I said, "Lack of sex appeal?"

Chloe snorted. "Doesn't strike me as very *sex appealing*, going round like a bunch of animated candyfloss."

What on earth was she talking about?

"That hair," said Chloe. "All puffed up. And that ridiculous top! I couldn't decide whether it was meant to be on the shoulder or off."

Mostly it had been off. Quite a long way off. I had watched Danny's eyes, going round like Catherine wheels.

"And *did* you see those boots?"

Boots? I froze. What boots? My boots?

55

"What was wrong with them?" I said.

"Tart boots," said Chloe. She giggled. "That's what my mum called them!"

Chloe's mum was obviously an idiot. What did she know? I huffed, grumpily, into the phone.

"What's going on?" said Chloe. "You sound all humpish."

I said, "I'm tired."

"*Tired?* Really? I'm so wide awake I could stay up all night! Listen, I was thinking, if Dee's out of hospital—"

"She is," I said.

"Oh." Chloe sounded surprised. "How do you know? Did you ring?"

"No, I mean... she's *probably* out of hospital. I mean, she usually is. When she goes in. She usually comes out next day. I mean, like – well! She's never in for more than one night. You know?" I was growing more flustered by the second. I didn't want even Chloe to know how stupid I'd been. If Chloe knew, she would tell Dee for sure, because Chloe is quite incapable of keeping a secret, and I certainly didn't want Dee knowing. It would only upset her.

"Well! I'll ring and find out," said Chloe. "If she's home, shall we go and see her?"

I mumbled, "Could, I s'ppose."

"We ought," said Chloe. "She'll be dying to know how it went!"

"You could both come round here," I said.

"It'd be better if we went to her place."

I sighed. "All right."

"You're sounding all humpish again," said Chloe. "It's not Mel, is it? You're not letting her get to you? She is just so *nothing*. She's rubbish! Don't worry about her."

I wasn't worried about Mel, I was worried about going round to visit Dee and bumping into her brother. What would I say? What would I do? I didn't ever want to set eyes on him again!

"Let's go tomorrow morning," said Chloe. "I'll text you."

I said OK, but my brain was whirring furiously,

thinking of what excuses I could make. I would have to be ill! Or going somewhere with Mum. Or the dentist, or the doctor, or just anywhere. I couldn't face the thought of seeing Dee! Except... I would have to see her some time. We were always going round to each other's places. I couldn't just suddenly stop. She would think I didn't want to be friends with her any more. I didn't know what to do!

Seconds after Chloe rang off, the phone started up again. It was Dee...

"Oh!" she said. "You're back!"

58

Trying hard to sound bright and cheery, I said, "Nine o'clock curfew."

"Yes, but what happened? Paul was worried about you! He said he was giving you a lift and you jumped out of the car. What d'you go and do that for?"

She sounded reproachful. More than reproachful: she sounded quite cross. She had some nerve! She'd only got his side of the story; what about mine?

"Jo? What d'you go and jump out of the car for?"

I swallowed. "I s-suddenly realised... I'd left my phone in the restaurant."

"I know, Paul said. But he was going to take you back there! You might have given him a chance. He said you frightened the life out of him, tearing across the road like that."

How could I tell her that he had frightened the life out of me? He was her brother, and she probably loved him. When she'd introduced him to us, me and Chloe, that one time, she'd seemed, like, really proud. Like he was something special. Even if I told her why I'd jumped out of the car, she probably wouldn't believe me. She wouldn't believe that her beloved brother could kidnap someone. Because that *was* what he'd done. Dee would say I was imagining it. But I wasn't! He'd deliberately driven the wrong way. How would she explain that? And the screwdriver in the glove compartment? And pretending not to have a mobile phone! Everyone had a mobile phone. If I hadn't left mine in the restaurant, if I'd had it with me and I'd tried to use it, he would never have let me. He would never have let me ring home! If it hadn't been for the traffic lights being on red, I would never have got home. Mum would have waited and waited for me, getting more and more distraught, until in the end she would have had to call the police. And then it would have been on television, and in the papers. *Has anyone seen this girl?* And poor Mum, weeping, as she begged whoever had taken me to let me go. Only by then it would be too late. And one day somebody walking a dog round the gravelpits would come across a body, and it would Mum's worst nightmare come true. But how could I explain any of this to Dee?

"*Jo?*" The way she said it, it was like... accusing. Like I was the one who'd done something wrong, upsetting her brother. I was quite surprised that he had mentioned it to her. I would have thought he'd have wanted to keep quiet about it, but no doubt he'd decided it was best to get in first and make like he was the injured party, in case I reported him, or anything. Not that I would. I still desperately didn't want Mum finding out.

"Jo, are you there?" She was getting impatient, now. "Say something! Don't just go all quiet on me!"

"Look, I'm really tired," I said. "I want to go to bed."

"Just tell me why you ran off like that!"

"I don't know! I wasn't thinking. I just saw this bus and... I had to get my phone! I've already lost two, Mum would have gone spare."

"But Paul would have *taken* you."

"I didn't want to put him to any trouble," I said. "Anyway, it's OK, 'cos I got the phone back. I've just been speaking to Chloe, and she said she's going to ring you and see if you're home. Which you obviously are," I said, brightly, though I wasn't actually feeling bright, I was feeling quite limp and weak; with shock, I suppose. Thinking of Mum sitting at home waiting for me had brought back all the horror of being in that car and knowing that I had made this terrible mistake. "You are home," I said, "aren't you?"

"Yes, of course I am!" snapped Dee. "Paul told you I was."

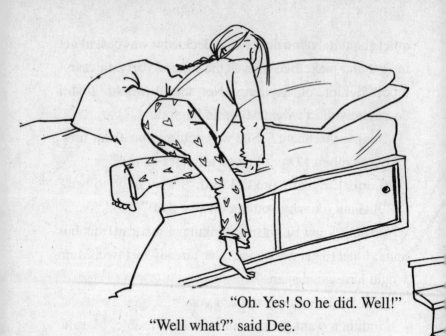

"Oh. Yes! So he did. Well!"

"Well what?" said Dee.

"I hope you're feeling better," I said. But Dee just made an exasperated sound and rang off.

I really hated falling out with Dee, but I just didn't know what to say to her. Also, to be honest, I couldn't understand what her problem was. So I'd jumped out of the car and leapt on to a bus. So what? It hardly seemed any good reason for her to be mad at me. What could he have said to make her so mad? Maybe he'd told her how I'd nearly made him crash the car. That would make her mad. The thought of me, putting him in danger. *Me*, putting *him* in danger! It was sick. Sick, sick, *sick*. And there wasn't a thing I could do to put it right. I couldn't tell Dee that it was him, her precious brother, leaning over me, opening the glove compartment. *Reaching for the screwdriver.* If I hadn't lurched sideways and thrown him off balance—

"Jo?"

Oh no, it was Mum calling up the stairs! She'd obviously got rid of the Handkerchief Lady. I sprang into bed, trying to make like I'd gone to sleep and forgotten to switch the light off, but Mum is almost never fooled by any of my ruses. She can see straight through me! I guess it's what comes of having a mum who's psychic.

"Jo?" She stuck her head round the door. "You still awake?"

Of course she knew I was! But I made this big production of suddenly waking up with a start.

"Oh," I said, "has it gone?"

"Miss Allardyce? Yes. She only needed a little pepping up. Now, then!" Mum folded her arms; a sure sign she meant business. "What happened, young lady?"

"Woman," I said.

"*Girl*," said Mum. "*Teenage* girl. Gave me her word she would be back by nine."

"I got back by twenty past," I bleated. "And I did ring you!"

"You think that makes it all right?" said Mum.

"I couldn't help it! I couldn't get through. I told you... they were engaged!"

"For half an hour?"

I blinked. "Well... y-yes."

"Rubbish! You're not telling me the line was busy right through from eight thirty till nine o'clock?"

"Maybe not qu-quite from eight thirty," I mumbled.

"Joanne, just be honest! You didn't even try ringing until nine o'clock, did you?"

I huddled down beneath the duvet, trying to escape the wrath that was to come. Mum is actually quite tolerant, but oh, boy! When she blows, she really blows. I braced myself for the tirade. *The last time I shall trust you, in future you'll be treated like a child, never allowed out by yourself at night again...*

"Oh, I can't be bothered!" said Mum. She threw her arms into the air, then pressed both hands on top of her head, as if to keep it from blasting off. "I've had a really tiring day. The last thing I need right now is my own daughter giving me a load of hassle."

I wriggled my way back out of the duvet. "I'm sorry, Mum! I am... really I am!"

"Bit late for that," grumbled Mum. But she was

softening, I could tell. I crept closer and stretched out a finger, trying to wipe away her frown lines.

"You won't get round me like that," said Mum. "You seem to think I'm just a stupid old fusspot, but the fact is, it's not safe out there for a young girl on her own at night. And don't start pulling faces at me!"

I wasn't pulling faces. I'd learnt my lesson! I wouldn't pull faces ever again.

"Mum." I settled myself, cross-legged in the bed. "You don't think you're working too hard, do you?"

"Well, of course I am," said Mum. "It's the only way I know how to make a living."

"But Dad pays you something!"

"Yes, your dad is quite generous."

"It's not like we're on the breadline, or anything."

"No; but I have to contribute my share."

"You don't have to wear yourself out!" I'd seen Mum at the end of some of her sessions; she would emerge looking absolutely drained. "I just don't know why you keep seeing that woman," I said.

"Who? Poor Miss Allardyce?"

"She's a neurotic!"

"She can't help it. She pays her money, the same as anyone else."

"Yes, and she wears you to a frazzle! She's like a *leech*. I can't understand why you bother with her."

"Someone has to bother. You can't ignore people's suffering."

"I can," I said. "When it's people like her, that latch on to you and take advantage of you and turn up at all hours of the day and night expecting you to just drop everything at a moment's notice and patch up their pathetic messy lives for them. It's just so *selfish*!"

"It is selfish," agreed Mum. "But that's all part and parcel of the condition."

I said, "What *condition*? I wouldn't get away with behaving like that!"

"No, you wouldn't," said Mum, "because you have no reason to." She said that Miss Allardyce was a "sad and troubled woman", but that things had happened in her life to make her as she was.

"Like what?" I said.

Mum wagged a finger. "Now, Jo! You know better than that."

I did, unfortunately. I was dying to hear what things had happened in the Handkerchief Lady's life, but I knew that Mum would never tell me. Everybody thinks of clairvoyants as being charlatans and frauds. They think it's all just play-acting, but Mum's gift is absolutely genuine, and Mum herself is one hundred per cent professional. She never gives away her clients' secrets. Maybe some day she'll write a book. Everybody in it would be anonymous, but I bet I'd be able to guess who some of them were! All she would say now was that I shouldn't make "superficial judgements".

"Things are not always what they seem. People are not always what they seem. The more you get to know a person, the more you understand – and the more you forgive."

I said, "Huh!"

"And what is that supposed to mean?" said Mum.

What it meant was, there were some people I didn't think could ever be forgiven. Some people I didn't think deserved to be forgiven. But I couldn't say this to Mum. She would immediately guess that I had someone particular in mind and would want to know who, and why, and what had happened. And even though, of course, I would deny it, Mum has an uncomfortable knack of ferreting out the truth.

"Do you forgive *me*?" I said. "For coming in late?"

"I'll have to think about that one," said Mum. "Ask me in the morning!"

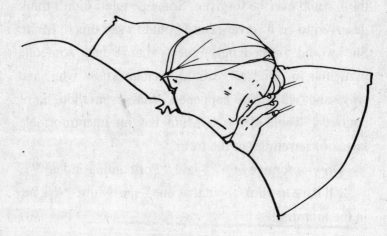

four

I HAD THE most horrible night. It was full of scary dreams, all about gravel pits. But I wasn't asleep! I wasn't awake, either; I just lay, stiff and cold, like a corpse, in some kind of limbo, where Paul's face kept looming at me, mushroom pale with colourless eyes, out of a swirling yellow mist, and his voice kept urging me to "Ring your mum! Why don't you?" but every time I reached out for my mobile, it wasn't there. Paul said, "How careless! You've thrown away your chances. You'll never get home now." I cried, "But I must! I must get back to Mum!" So then he told me that there might be a phone in the glove compartment, and he reached across me to get at it, and I screamed, and the car veered across the road, and I struggled to open the door, but it wouldn't open, and Paul just laughed, this gloating laugh, and went on driving towards the gravel pits.

The dream never went any further; we never actually reached the gravel pits. But I knew all the time that they were there, waiting for me, at the bottom of the hill; and I knew that something evil was waiting there with them. If we ever did reach those gravel pits, I wouldn't be coming back.

Over and over, the dream repeated itself, like a loop of film, until I felt like I was going mad. In the end I must have fallen asleep, because at half past eight I woke up with a rude start when Mum came banging at the door wanting to know if I ever intended to get up. I was just so relieved when I heard her voice and realised that I was safe in my bed, and not trapped in Paul's car! I yelled at Mum that I was coming, and she said, "About time, too! Sleeping your life away."

I felt a whole lot stronger once I was up and dressed. I even began to wonder if perhaps I had exaggerated the whole incident. I am not one of those people (like Chloe, for example) who loves to dramatise everything, but maybe I had... overreacted. Maybe. At any rate, when Chloe rang me just after breakfast, saying had I got her text message and how about we go round to Dee's that afternoon, I didn't immediately fly into a panic and start burbling about dentist's appointments or having to go somewhere with Mum. I thought to myself that sooner or later I would have to go round to Dee's, because whatever her brother might be, Dee herself was still my friend, and the longer I left it the more difficult it would be to patch up our little disagreement. It wasn't a quarrel! But we had both been tetchy, and I didn't like being tetchy with Dee. So I told Chloe that after lunch would be fine, and we agreed to meet up at two o'clock, round Dee's place. Chloe said that she had already rung Dee to check it would be OK. I asked her what Dee had said.

"She said yes," said Chloe. "It'd be OK."

"Did you tell her we'd both be coming?"

"Course I did! I said I was going to ring you."

"What did she say when you said that?"

"She didn't say anything," said Chloe. "Why? What d'you think she should have said?"

"Oh! I dunno. I just wondered."

"Wondered what?"

"If she'd, like... said anything."

There was a pause. I could picture Chloe holding the phone away from her and pulling one of her faces. She had this habit, when anyone said something she thought a bit weird, of  crinkling her forehead and screwing her nose up, like a corkscrew. I suppose I was being a bit weird, only I had to check that Dee really did want me to go round. She'd been so cross on the phone! So angry with me for running out on her brother. But I couldn't go into the details with Chloe, so I just said again that I would see her at two and left her to go on pulling faces.

Usually when we went round to Dee's we shut ourselves up in her bedroom so we could be private, but Dee's bedroom is way up the top of the house, in what used to be the attic, and her mum said she wasn't yet well enough to "do stairs".

"But don't worry! You can have the front room all to yourselves. I won't come and pry."

Dee's mum is so lovely! It made me feel really bad, thinking all those dreadful thoughts about her son. Not that he was, actually, her son; he belonged to her husband. Dee's dad is heaps older than her mum. But that time when we'd been introduced to Paul, Dee's mum had been there, and she'd had her arm round his shoulders like she was really fond of him. It would be a terrible shock, if I were to reveal what he had done. She would be devastated to think that he might be a hideous prowling monster, preying on young girls, and her knowing nothing about it. Not even suspecting. I couldn't do it to her! Nor to Dee. It just confirmed my belief that it would be far the best thing for everyone, not only for me, but for Dee's family as well, if I didn't say anything. Which to be honest was a huge relief, as I thought that I would far rather just put it behind me and try to pretend that it had never happened.

Something else which was a huge relief: Dee seemed to have forgotten that she was upset with me. She was eager to hear how the celebration had gone, so for the next half hour we sat around cosily discussing it, with me and Chloe telling her what everyone had been wearing, and how utterly ghastly Mel Sanders had been, and what a complete idiot she'd made of herself.

"Trying to get it off with every guy that came anywhere near us!"

"She even tried it on with some old bloke behind the bar."

"Yes, and he must have been at least fifty!"

"It was just *so* degrading."

"Pathetic, if you ask me."

"And you should have seen what she was wearing! Those *boots*." Chloe sprang up and began tottering across the room on the tips of her toes with her knees bowed. "Tart boots!"

"Actually, they're glitter boots," I said.

"They're what?"

"Glitter boots!"

"Tart boots."

"Gl—"

"Never mind about the boots," said Dee. "Tell me about Danny!"

I subsided, glumly, into a nest of cushions on the sofa. "Nothing to tell."

"Why not? Didn't you see him?"

"She saw him, but he didn't see her," said Chloe. "All anyone could look at was Mel in her tart boots!"

"Really?" Dee gazed at me, sympathetically.

"It wasn't his fault," I said. "She hypnotises them!"

"So you didn't get to speak to him?"

I shook my head.

"Oh, Jo! And that was the whole point of it!"

"I know," I said. "But what can you do?"

"Buy a pair of tart boots!" said Chloe, and guffawed.

"Shut up," said Dee. "This is serious! I've got an idea... why don't we go there by ourselves? Just the three of us? Then he'll *have* to take notice."

Chloe said, "Brilliant! When shall we do it?"

"After Christmas?" said Dee.

"Yes, then we could tell our parents it was a going-back-to-school celebration. They'd like that... the thought we were all so eager to get back and start working again!"

"All right," said Dee. "Let's go for it!"

"Jo?" Chloe poked at me. "You on?"

"I am if Mum will let me," I said. "She doesn't really like me being out at night."

"Especially when you're late back," said Dee.

"*Late?*" said Chloe. "*Were* you?"

77

I said, "Only a little bit."

"But you left so early! You left loads before I did. I wondered where you'd gone, you just disappeared. I looked for you, and someone said you'd rushed off."

"I went to get the bus," I said.

"*Bus?*"

"Yes, you know," I said. "One of those red things with lots of seats inside? Maybe you've never been on one."

"Wouldn't want to go on one! Not at that time of night. Anyway, I thought you said your mum told you to get a cab? From *Albert*."

Chloe knew all about Albert, and how he mother-henned me. So did Dee; they used to tease me about it.

"I couldn't get through," I said. I crossed my fingers as I said it. I certainly wasn't admitting to Chloe that I'd been trying to save money for a pair of glitter boots. As a matter of fact, I was fast going off the whole idea of glitter boots. I wished I'd never set eyes on the wretched things! If I hadn't known about them, I wouldn't have wanted them, and the nightmare of last night would never have happened.

"You should have waited for me," said Chloe. "My dad would've given you a lift. He wouldn't have minded!"

"Paul gave her one," said Dee. "He saw her standing there and he knew it wasn't safe, so he *very kindly*" – she glared at me – "out of the *goodness of his heart*, offered to take her all the way home."

She was still mad at me. Even though she seemed friendly enough on the surface, she was obviously seething underneath. It was so unfair! I felt like shouting at her. "Your precious tried to abduct me!" But I couldn't. I just couldn't do it to her. And, in any case, there was Mum.

Chloe was looking from one to the other of us. She has these antennae like a bat's radar, they pick up the least little thing.

"So what happened?" She leaned forward, eagerly.

"Nothing happened." I got in fast, ahead of Dee. "I just left my phone in the restaurant and had to go back and get it."

"He'd have *taken* you!" shrieked Dee. She was like one of those old gramophones, when the needle gets stuck. He'd have taken you, he'd have taken you, he'd have taken you. Chloe, by now, was all bright-eyed and alert, on the scent of some good gossip. She loves a bit of goss. I think it would be true to say that she thrives on it.

"Look," I said, "just don't keep on."

"But you were such an *idiot*!"

"Why? Why?" Chloe's ears were practically flapping in the breeze. "What did she do?"

"I didn't do anything! I just—"

"Just nearly went and gave Paul a heart attack! Jumping out of the car like that."

"You jumped out of the *car*?"

"We stopped at the lights," I said, "and there just happened to be a bus coming, so *to save him having to go all the way back*" – it was my turn to glare at Dee – "I rushed off and got it. OK? Simple!"

"You got the bus?"

"*Yes.*" I did wish she would stop repeating everything. It was beginning to get on my nerves. "What would you have done?"

"I'd have asked him to take me," said Chloe.

"Anyone would, that had any sense," said Dee. "I mean, honestly! How d'you think Paul would've felt, having to tell your mum you'd got run over?"

That was too much. That was more than I could take. I opened my mouth to yell the truth at her – and then promptly closed it again, just in time, as the door opened. I thought it was going to be Dee's mum, but it wasn't; it was *him*. Paul. He was really thrown when he saw me sitting there. I could tell, from the way he coloured up.

"Sorry," he said. "Sorry! I didn't realise."

"It's OK," said Dee. "You can come in."

Chloe giggled. "We're decent!"

"Actually, we were just going," I said.

Chloe did the corkscrew thing with her nose. "We were?"

I certainly was; I couldn't bear to be in the same room with him. "I've got to get home," I said. Reluctantly, Chloe unwrapped herself from the cushion she'd been hugging and scrambled to her feet.

"I suppose I'd better come."

"You don't have to go on my account," said Paul. "I only came to fetch something."

"'S OK," said Chloe. "I told Mum I'd be back by four."

He stood, holding the door for us. As I walked past he said, "I take it you got home all right in the end?"

82

Stiffly I said, "Yes, thank you."

"And you got your phone?"

"Yes."

"Good!"

There was a pause. I knew Dee was waiting for me to apologise to him, to say how sorry I was for behaving like an idiot and nearly giving him a heart attack, but not even for the sake of our friendship was I prepared to do that. I just couldn't bring myself.

"Paul's really nice, isn't he?" said Chloe, as we set off down the road together. Fortunately, I was spared having to reply as she simply rushed straight on. "Wish I'd got a brother like that!"

It's true that Chloe's brother Jude, who is five years older than her, was like something out of the dark ages, when men were men and women were doormats, and that his

greatest delight in life was roaring round the estate on his motorbike, frightening old ladies and generally upsetting people; but at least he didn't abduct young girls.

"Could you fancy him?" She giggled. "I could."

Not me. No thank you! I supposed he wasn't bad looking if you happened to go for blond men (which I didn't, and never have). A bit like an older version of Dee, with the same silvery fair hair and blue eyes, except that Dee's eyes are bright, like the sky on a summer day, while his were pale and somehow wishy washy. I said this to Chloe, who said, "*I* could go for him!"

"I wouldn't, if I were you," I said.

"Why not?" Chloe was on it, immediately. What did I know that she didn't? "Is he married?"

I said, "No idea, but he's loads too old."

"Mm... kind of mysterious. Do you reckon he's got a past?"

I said, "Yes – he's probably been married six times and has a dozen kids. Listen, when you next see my mum, don't say anything about last night, will you? 'Cos if she knew I'd got the bus she'd never let me go anywhere, ever again!"

Chloe promised faithfully that she wouldn't breathe a word, and I knew that she meant it; but I also knew that she really couldn't be trusted. She makes these promises, thinking that she would die sooner than break them, and then at the first opportunity she goes and blabs. She is just totally incapable of keeping quiet. I decided that I would do my best to keep her and Mum well apart for at least the new few weeks...

five

I HAVE ALWAYS thought of myself as quite a stolid sort of person. By which I mean that I am pretty grounded, not necessarily that I am boring and unimaginative. Though it is true that my imagination is nowhere near as vivid as Chloe's. Hers tends to splatter and splurge all over the place. "Running rampant", as one of our teachers once said, when Chloe terrified the life out of most of us by claiming to have seen a headless ghost lurking in the lower-school changing rooms.

"It wasn't just headless, it was knickerless, too!"

That was when Miss Mitchell accused her of letting her imagination "run rampant". My imagination does *not* run rampant. I have never seen any headless ghosts, with or without knickers. In fact, I have never seen a ghost of any kind, unless you count the time I saw my gran dancing with my grandad when they were young; but that was more of a recall. A vision from the past. As opposed to a *manifestation*. Gran wasn't actually there, in front of me. And far from finding it frightening, I laughed and felt happy.

What I'm saying is, I am definitely not a nervous type. I am not, for instance, scared of the dark, which I know a lot of people are; and when I went to the waxworks with my Auntie Sue and my cousin Posy and saw the Chamber of Horrors, it didn't bother me one little bit. Posy was all shaking, and clutching her mum's hand, but I was just, like, really interested. Same when Mum took us to a theme park and we went on the Ghost Ride. Posy screamed fit to bust! I screamed, too, but I only did it for fun. I'd have gone on it again, no problem. As for the London Dungeon... me and Chloe shrieked and giggled all the way round it.

So like I say, I am not a nervous type; but the events of that night continued to haunt me. I think it was the first time in my life that I had ever been truly frightened. It got so that I was reluctant to go to bed, for fear of what would happen when I closed my eyes. I started staying up later and later, watching telly into the small hours, until Mum caught me at it and demanded to know what I thought I was doing.

"Mum, it's holiday time!" I said.

Mum said holiday time or not, I ought to know better.

"Just taking advantage!" she said. "Your poor old mum crashes out at ten o'clock because she's totally shattered, and you sit here square-eyed half way through the night watching heaven knows what unsuitable rubbish!"

I hardly knew what I was watching, to tell the truth; I just didn't want to go to bed and have bad dreams. But after that I couldn't watch telly, because Mum made me promise – "No sneaking out of bed the minute my back's turned, do you hear me?" – so all I had was books, which are great for lying down and going to sleep with but no good at all for keeping awake as your eyelids very quickly grow heavy and start drooping, and before you know it you've gone and lost consciousness. And then the dreams begin, and there is nothing you can do about it.

Mum and me spent Christmas like we always do, with Auntie Sue and Uncle Frank, and my cousin Posy. I love Auntie Sue and Uncle Frank, but Posy is a bit of a trial. We are almost the same age, and so, of course, our mums expect us to do things together and be all cosy and chummy and talk girl talk in her bedroom. Well, sorry, I hate to ruin this idyllic picture, but the fact is she and I have absolutely nothing whatsoever in common. Not one single, solitary thing. How can you talk girl talk with someone who has *no* interest in boys, *no* interest in clothes, *no* interest in music – well, not what I would call music. To give you an example, she once went to a Cliff Richard concert with her mum and dad!!! She said he was just "so lovely"! Pardon me while I go away to recover myself.

Right. OK. Where was I? Saying about Posy. Her main passion in life, her *only* passion in life, is playing the harp. She started off with a teeny tiny little one, and now she has graduated to a great whopping thing almost bigger than she is. I suppose one day she will be 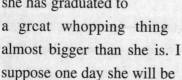 famous for her harp playing, and then I shall go round boasting to everyone that she is my cousin. In the meantime, if you happen to think, as I do, that the harp is an instrument the world could well do without, it does leave you a bit short of conversation. Mum says I should learn to be more tolerant.

"Live and let live. And don't you dare to sit there pulling faces while she's playing!"

To which I retort that a little plinking and plonking goes a long way, and why does it always, *always* have to be inflicted on us?

"Because her mum and dad are proud of her!" snaps Mum. "For goodness' sake, it's only once a year! Just put up with it."

Normally, as I am sure you will understand, I set out for Christmas with a glum and sinking feeling in the pit of my stomach. This Christmas – which just shows the state I was in – I was only too relieved to be getting away. Sooner Posy and her heavenly harp than run the risk of bumping into Paul every time I set foot outside the front door. I was also hoping that being in a totally different part of the world, down in Somerset, would put a stop to the bad dreams, and I have to say that it did help.

We came back home the day after Boxing Day and I thought that perhaps I was cured and could start living normally again, but it seems that when you have had a really bad fright it is not so easy to get over it. It's like there's a kind of aftershock. I wasn't having the dreams any more, and that was a relief, but when Dee rang up to check that I was going to the New Year firework display with her as usual, I desperately didn't want to go. Dee couldn't understand it, and neither could Mum. Mum said, "But you always go to the fireworks! What's the matter? You and Dee haven't fallen out, have you?"

I told her no, which was true. Dee had sounded her old self when she rang, not a hint of irritation. She had obviously forgiven me, and just wanted to be friends again.

"So why don't you want to go?" said Mum.

I hunched a shoulder and muttered that I didn't know. "I just don't."

"Oh, now, come on! There must be a reason. Something you're not telling me."

I sucked in my cheeks and looked down, hard, at the floor. It's fortunate that Mum made this vow, when I was little, that she would never, ever use her gift on me, a bit like doctors not treating members of their own family. She could have done it, quite easily. But she wouldn't, because that would have been like invading my privacy.

She tried coaxing me. She said, again, "Jo, you always go!"

"Twice," I said. "I've been *twice*."

"And you've enjoyed it. You've had fun!"

So why didn't Mum go if she thought it was so great? I muttered this under my breath, not intending Mum to hear. I didn't think she had, because she didn't pick up on it. Instead, in worried tones, she said, "You always *told* me you had fun."

"Yeah?" I said this in my best swaggering sort of voice. It seemed to me that a bit of bravado was called for, if I didn't want Mum probing too deeply. "So I've changed my mind. I've gone off the idea."

"Gone off the idea of fireworks?"

"Yeah. Right! You grow out of things, you know? I just happen to have grown out of fireworks."

It was a gross lie, 'cos I love those fireworks parties. But I was just so scared that *he* would be there. And it would be dark, and there would be crowds of people. It's all too easy to get lost in crowds of people. Worst of all, it was in Water Tower Park. Water Tower Park is right opposite the gravel pits, at the bottom of Gravelpit Hill. If there was one place in the world I didn't ever want to go to, that was it: Gravelpit Hill. Even just the sound of it made my insides start shaking.

One of the drawbacks of having a mum who is psychic is that you cannot get away with all the little fibs and evasions that most people take for granted. Mum always knows when I'm not telling her the truth.

"Something's happened," she said. "Something's upset you. It's all right, I'm not going to ask you what it is; I'm sure you'd tell me if you wanted me to know. Why don't we go along together?"

That stopped me *right* in my tracks. Go along together? To a fireworks display? Mum hates fireworks!

"You were absolutely right," she said. "I ought to go." So she had heard me. Trust Mum! Ears like a lynx.

"What do you say? It's New Year's Eve! You can't sit at home all by yourself."

"You would have done," I said.

"Oh, well! Me. I'm old," said Mum.

She isn't old! Forty isn't old. But Mum is not a great one for going out and socialising; it was one of the things that she and Dad always used to fall out about. Dad just loves to party! Maybe it is being psychic that makes Mum such a home body. She gets too many... messages, too many emotions, when she is among people. But I am psychic, too, and I am certainly not a home body! Not as a rule, I'm not.

Mum obviously sensed that I was still dithering.

"You and me," she said. "We'll go together. It's time we did something together. We'll have fun!"

I couldn't help being apprehensive, even with Mum for company. I tried hard to relax, and laugh, and make like I was having a good time. I felt I owed it to Mum. I knew she had only come because she wanted me to enjoy myself, and that really she would have been far happier tucked up at home with a book and a glass of wine. So I grinned like mad, and waved at people I knew, and shouted "Hi!" and went *ooh* and *aaah* as the rockets exploded, but all the time I pressed close to Mum, like I used to when I was little and was scared she might suddenly disappear.

95

Dee was there with her mum and dad, and we all stood together for a bit and chatted.

"I thought you weren't going to come?" said Dee.

I said, "I wasn't. I was going to stay in with Mum."

"You can't stay in on New Year's Eve!" said Dee.

"I know, that's what Mum said."

"Chloe's around somewhere, but I haven't seen her. Have you?"

I shook my head. I did so hope she wasn't going to suggest we went off by ourselves to look for her. I wanted to ask if Paul was here, but I couldn't bring myself to say his name. In the end, Dee's mum and dad moved off to talk to someone else, and Dee went with them, leaving me still stuck like a limpet to Mum's side. I wished I'd had the courage to ask about her brother! Not knowing was even worse than knowing. I kept imagining him lingering and loitering, out in the darkness, at the edge of the crowd. I don't think I was ever more glad of anything than when the clock at last struck twelve, and we could sing Auld Lang Syne and go home. I felt safe at home; I hadn't felt safe in Water Tower Park. Mum asked me if I'd enjoyed myself, and of course I said yes. I don't think she altogether believed me, but she didn't say anything. Mum is *so* scrupulous about not prying. I guess it's because she knows she could probe my emotions any time she wanted, and there would be nothing I could do to stop her. The result is, I probably have more secrets from her than I would if she was just an ordinary mum.

Just occasionally I have wished that Mum *could* be a more ordinary mum, so that she would feel free to dig and delve and nag like they do. *What are you keeping from me? What aren't you telling me?* I think if she hadn't had her clairvoyant gift she might have got the truth out of me. And oh, in some ways, it would have been such a relief! To have been forced into telling her. It would have been like... handing over the burden. As it was, I kept it all to myself. Sometimes I thought it was growing easier; then something would happen to set it all off again.

The previous year, after Christmas, I'd gone up to Birmingham to stay with Dad and Irene for a few days, and Dad was expecting me to do the same this year. I wanted to go, 'cos I wanted to see Dad, but suddenly I found I was having nightmares about getting there. I'd been so proud last year setting off on the train all by myself. I'd begged Mum to let me do it, so now, of course, she took it for granted that I'd want to do it again. But the bad dreams had come back, except that now it was a train I was trapped on. I kept trying to find the communication cord, and I couldn't, and it was just so scary!

I didn't say anything to Mum about it. I'd looked in her diary and seen that she had two bookings for the day

I was due to travel, and I knew I couldn't ask her to cancel them, just to drive me up to Birmingham. In the end I was glad that I didn't, in spite of the nightmares, because once I was actually on the train, and surrounded by people, all my fears fell away from me and I thought how silly and exaggerated they were.

It was lovely being with Dad again. It is quite a different experience from being with Mum, as they are almost exact opposites. Mum is quiet and serious, whereas Dad is very bright and extrovert. Also, he is a touchy-feely kind of person, which Mum is not. I am not sure that I am, either, to tell the truth, but I do like it when Dad envelops me in a big squeezy hug.

Me and Mum peck each other on the cheek occasionally, but that is about all. I don't know how she and Dad ever got it together! How did two people who are so entirely different ever think that they were soul mates? But they obviously were, once; and they are still good friends and care about each other.

I know lots of people whose mums and dads have split up and are really mean and vicious to each other and hardly even talk. I would just hate that! Mum and Dad speak quite often on the phone, and whenever I go to Birmingham Dad always wants to know how Mum is, just like when I get back the first thing Mum says is, "How's your Dad?" If people must split up, although I think it is terribly sad, then this is probably the way to do it.

It helps that Irene is a really nice person, very warm and friendly, so that I don't bear her any grudges for taking Mum's place. Unlike Mum, who enjoys her own company, Dad could not have survived by himself. He needs someone to kiss and cuddle and be there for him. Irene is rather billowy, with big soft wobbly bosoms, so I should think she cuddles really well!

I felt good when I got back home. I felt that at last I really had recovered myself; that from now on there would be no bad dreams, no more panics. I had learnt my lesson. Never again would I be stupid enough to get into a car with someone I didn't properly know. I'd been lucky to escape, but I *had* escaped, and now it was time to put it all behind me and move on. Yeah!

On our last Friday before the new term started, we had our going-back-to-school celebration in the Pizza Palace. Mum had said she was most impressed by my desire to get back to my lessons, but she would really rather I didn't go out by myself at night again.

"Not after last time. I don't want to seem like a harridan, but you were almost half an hour late. So if you don't mind, I think we'll keep it to a middle-of-the-day affair."

I didn't even try to argue with her. I told the others that it was lunch time or nothing, and they were quite happy.

"I know he works lunches," said Chloe. "I've seen him!"

"Yes, and there won't be so much competition at that time of day," said Dee.

One way and another, I'd had quite a lot of money for Christmas. Dad had given me a cheque and Irene had given me a really cool top, black with red swirls

101

(Mum said, "Hm! Rather sophisticated," in tones that weren't altogether approving, but personally I thought it was brilliant. Irene has great taste!). From Auntie Sue and Uncle Frank I'd had gift vouchers for the Body Shop; Gran-up-North had sent real money, by Special Delivery. I just love real money! Mum had told me that I could spend "up to £25" on her Beattie's store card, "Since clothes seem the only thing you care about."

Not true! I care about lots of things, such as, for example, protecting the environment and Save the Children. I am *always* putting money in collecting boxes. But obviously clothes are important and I did think I was entitled to a bit of a spending spree before going back to the daily grind of lessons and homework. I bought some black trousers, to go with my new black top, hesitated over a  miniskirt, decided against – Mum heaved a sigh of relief – tried on a couple of dresses, both unutterably hideous, went back and bought the miniskirt.

"You'd get away far cheaper just buying a scarf," said Mum.

I said, "What do I want a scarf for? I want a skirt!"

Mum said that if I tied a scarf round my waist, I would have a skirt.

"And it would probably cover up a great deal more of you than that thing does!"

Aha! She was just worried that people would be able to see my knickers.

"I'll only wear it for *parties*," I said.

"Like that makes it all right?" said Mum.

Sometimes I think that maybe forty is quite old, after all. I pointed out to Mum that when we had gone on holiday I'd worn a bikini.

"That didn't seem to bother you!"

"It did," said Mum, "but I knew I'd be fighting a losing battle. Can we go home now, or do you want to fritter more money away?"

I said that I wanted to fritter, so we ambled through the shopping centre, finally fetching up at the shop where I'd seen the glitter boots. They were still there, glittering away, but somehow they seemed to have lost their charm. They seemed a bit... tacky. So I bought a pair of PVC ones, instead. Bright red, with straps.

"Won't last five minutes," said Mum.

She says that about everything. She's always right, of course, but she misses the point. Who *needs* things to last five minutes? Mum has stuff in her wardrobe that she bought years ago. I don't know how she can bear to be seen in it!

It was fun, having our back-to-school celebration. Just the three of us – and gorgeous Danny! Without that idiotic Mel to distract him, he actually recognised me and remembered who I was.

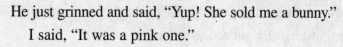

"Oh!" he said. "You're the one who sold me the bunny!"

Chloe, needless to say, instantly dissolved into giggles. I felt like slapping her, but fortunately Danny didn't seem to be embarrassed by her ridiculous behaviour.

He just grinned and said, "Yup! She sold me a bunny."

I said, "It was a pink one."

"It was," said Danny. "It was a pink bunny."

Chloe said, "Wow!" and went off into yet another peal of mindless giggles.

"You can say wow," said Danny, "but it's not everybody that could sell me a pink bunny!"

I thought, *so there*, and kicked at Chloe under the table.

"Well!" Dee flopped herself against me, as Danny went off to take someone else's order. She let her head loll on my shoulder. "If that isn't cause for celebration, I don't know what is!"

I felt this big foolish beam spread across my face. Danny had remembered me! We had talked! We had had a conversation!

"Oh, boy," said Chloe. "She's got it really bad!"

I think I would have gone on foolishly beaming all the way home if the door of the restaurant hadn't suddenly swung open and Paul come walking in. I immediately froze. What was he doing here? It was Dee's mum who'd been going to collect us. She finished work at half past two, she'd said she'd be here to pick us up, I couldn't get into a car again with Paul!

"W-where's your m-mum?" I said.

"Oh, didn't I tell you?" said Dee. "Paul offered to come instead. We can give you a lift as well, if you like," she said to Chloe.

"It's OK," said Chloe. "Dad's coming."

That did it. I pushed back my chair and jumped up.

"I've suddenly remembered," I gabbled, "I told Mum I'd meet her in Beattie's. We're going to buy school stuff." I pulled a face. "*Boring*. But I'd better go, or she'll wonder where I am. See you Monday. Byeee!"

I flapped a hand and went rushing out, past a surprised-looking Paul, who said, "You're in a hurry!" Chloe came dashing after me, shrieking, "Jo! Your phone!" I'd gone and left it on the table again...

I snatched it from her, with muttered thanks, and ran like a hare all the way to the bus stop. I don't what I'd have done if Dee and Paul had driven past while I was waiting for the bus. Fortunately they didn't, as a bus came almost immediately; but I was shaking again, and that night the dreams came back. I began to wonder if I would ever be free of them, or whether they would haunt me for the rest of my life.

six

On Monday we went back to school. In spite of all our jokes about being *soooo* glad to start working again, and *soooo* glad to have mountains of homework – "Just *soooo* relieved I shan't have to sit watching telly all night" – I was actually quite happy to be back. With all its irritations (such as having to be in the same class as Mel Sanders, and play hockey in force ten gales), with all its silly little rules and regulations and its truly disgusting uniform (stripes!!! I ask you!), school was safe. School was *normal*. The worst that could happen to you at school was being sent to Mrs Jarvis (deputy head) for smoking in the games cupboard. Then, most probably, you would be suspended, as with any luck Mel Sanders would be before she was very much older. But since I almost threw up the only time I tried a fag, and since on the whole I am a reasonably law abiding sort of person, I really had nothing to worry about. Not even Paul.

I no longer froze at every corner, expecting him to be lurking there, nor jumped at every shadow. For a while I was nervous when out on the playing field because it is bordered by trees, and trees still made my knees turn to jelly, so that I did my best to stay safely in the middle, though this wasn't always possible, especially playing hockey. Miss Armstrong always liked to stick me way out on the wing, on account of me having these long gangly legs and her being of the mistaken opinion that this meant I enjoyed running. Unfortunately, having no aptitude *whatsoever* for the futile game of hockey, I generally managed to miss every pass that came my way, so that I was for ever cantering along by the side of the trees, with palpitating heart, in pursuit of that stupid little ball. And all the while, as I cantered, I would be thinking to myself how easily someone could be loitering there, in the shade of the

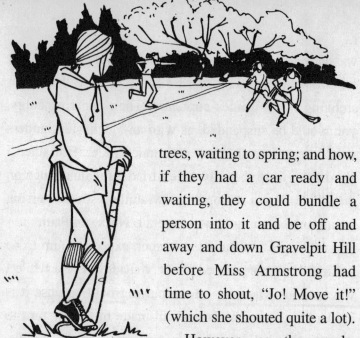

trees, waiting to spring; and how, if they had a car ready and waiting, they could bundle a person into it and be off and away and down Gravelpit Hill before Miss Armstrong had time to shout, "Jo! Move it!" (which she shouted quite a lot).

However, as the weeks passed by, and things jogged on just the same as always, too much homework, hockey in the freezing rain, Chloe told off a dozen times a day for talking, Mel Sanders sent home for customising her school uniform (i.e., hiking her skirt up practically to her navel), Dee being made class rep, me getting a D for a geography assignment – "Did you really expect to get away with this?" – quite honestly, in the end, I just didn't have the time to go on being neurotic. Little by little the bad dreams faded and I really did feel, at last, that I had come through my ordeal and could start living again.

Which I did!

We met up most Saturdays, the three of us, to mooch round the shopping centre. We had this thing where we pretended we were getting married, or going on holiday, or had a date with someone we really fancied, and we picked out all the clothes and accessories that we would buy. One Saturday we pretended we were pregnant and went to the Mother and Baby department, but Chloe kept getting these fits of the screaming giggles, which set me off, and even Dee, so that in the end we had to leave.

"Naked!" screeched Chloe. "We've got nothing to wear!"

Which, needless to say, set us off all over again. One Saturday we had a sleepover at Chloe's, where I was cajoled into playing The Game. I didn't really mind as we hadn't played it for ages. Not since that fateful night when we had decided to go for our end-of-term celebration. But it was all light-hearted. Chloe wanted me to do her and Dee.

"I can't remember when you last did us!"

So Chloe gave me her favourite silver bangle to hold, and Dee gave me her watch, and I did them both, sitting in torchlight in Chloe's bedroom. It was spooky, but it was fun. Whenever I did a session with Chloe it was like falling into a world made up of mad screen savers, all whirling and whizzing and scooting about. The inside of Chloe's mind never really stayed still long enough for me to make much sense of it. *Not* very restful. Dee, on the other hand, was more like the sea: calm on the surface, but waves building up below. I usually stayed on the surface as I really didn't want to probe too deeply; I didn't feel ready for that.

I had often wondered what I would say if, just by chance, I caught a glimpse of something really dark and disturbing. Would I tell them? Or would I keep quiet? I thought that I would probably keep quiet since, after all, it was only supposed to be a game. I suspected that Mum probably quite often saw things that were disturbing. I didn't know how she dealt with that as it wasn't something we had ever discussed, but I guessed that it must drain her and was one of the reasons she was so often worn out. It just added to my determination not to follow the same path that she had done. I mightn't mind helping people in some other kind of way, such as teaching handicapped children, say, or saving the rain forest, but no way was I going to plumb the depths of alien minds! I didn't even want to plumb the depths of my friends' minds.

"You never say anything bad, do you?" said Dee.

I replied, "Maybe that's because I don't see anything bad."

"That's right," said Chloe. "Because we're *happy*!"

We were happy, that term. We'd found our feet as Year 8s, and thought that we were pretty important; we'd got used to having Mrs Monahan as our class teacher, and had learnt all her little quirks and foibles. Like, for instance, the way she insisted that whenever she came into the room at the start of the day we all had to stand up and chant, "Good morning, Mrs Monahan!" Very weird, we thought; but a small price to pay for maintaining a good relationship.

Above all, of course, we had one another. Me and Chloe and Dee. We were so close, the three of us! Mel once sneeringly referred to us as "The Triplets". We didn't care. We were us, and she was no one. It is such a comfort, having friends! I was just so relieved that all the unpleasantness that had threatened us seemed to have blown over. More and more, it was like it had never been. I thought that we would be friends for ever.

And then it happened. The incident that shattered our lives: Gayle Gardiner went missing.

The news broke one Monday morning, the day we went back after half term. I first heard it on the radio (Mum won't let me watch breakfast TV. She's such a *puritan.*) As soon as they said the name Gayle Gardiner I just, like, froze.

"What's the matter?" said Mum.

I shrieked, "She's someone at school! She's in Year 12. Mum, put the telly on!"

I couldn't believe that it was *our* Gayle. But then Mum switched on to breakfast TV and I saw a picture of her, and all the familiar shivery darts of fear went zinging

through my body as I heard them say how she had gone off clubbing on Saturday evening with a friend, Ruby Simpson (who is also at our school),

but they had somehow or other managed to have a terrific row on the bus on the way in to town, with the result that Ruby had turned round and gone back home, leaving Gayle to go on to the club by herself. The trouble was that nobody who was at the club that night could remember seeing her, so that it was now believed she had never reached it; in which case, something must have happened to her between Hindes Corner, where she would have got off the bus, and Valley Road, just five minutes away, where the club was.

Hindes Corner was the last stop before the bus station and people had come forward to say they remembered her getting off, but nobody had noticed where she had gone after that, whether she had taken the short cut to Valley Road up the side of Marks & Spencer and out through the multistorey (which I certainly wouldn't have done) or whether she had gone the long way round, via the High Street.

If she'd gone by the High Street, there must have been loads of people about, or so I would have thought. The multistorey would have been too scary for words, but I could see that if you'd just had a humongous row with your best friend and were still sizzling with fury, then the adrenalin would be pumping round your body at such a rate you might well go boldly marching into the bowels of darkness thinking you were immune. It's the sort of stupid, reckless thing I could have done myself, once upon a time. I wouldn't now, because I'd learnt my lesson; I'd been lucky. But I looked at the picture of Gayle on breakfast TV, happy and laughing and full of life, and I knew, with a sickening sensation of clamminess down in the pit of my stomach, that whatever had happened to her could all too easily have happened to me.

The police were appealing for witnesses to come forward. I thought that someone surely must remember seeing her. It wasn't like she was one of those frowsy, mouselike people. She was really striking, she had this startling red gold hair, all frizzed out like a halo, she'd been wearing (this is what they said on the TV) a bright orange-and-black checked coat with a tartan miniskirt and long red boots.

"She couldn't just disappear," I said. I could hear my voice, all plaintive and appealing. "Not in the middle of a town!"

"It's been thirty-six hours," said Mum.

"Yes, but they've only just announced it. Someone's bound to have seen her."

Mum shook her head. Not like she was contradicting me; more like... despairing.

"The first twenty-four hours are the crucial ones."

I wasn't brave enough to ask her why; in any case, I already knew the answer. If a person isn't found in the first twenty-four hours, it usually means it's too late. Unless, of course, she'd simply run away from home.

I suggested this to Mum, who agreed that it was a possibility.

"I mean, she's in Year 12," I said. "She could have gone off with a boyfriend."

 Or she could have had a row with her parents. Mum agreed that that, too, was a possibility.

"But fancy letting a girl of that age go clubbing!"

"Mum, she's Year *12*," I said.

"Oh, I know, I know," said Mum. "You think I live in the dark ages, you think I'm just an old fusspot... but how do you imagine her mum and dad are feeling right now?"

Next day, we all knew how her mum and dad were feeling because they were on television, pleading for Gayle to come home. Or, if someone was holding her, to let her go and not hurt her. Both her mum and her dad were crying, and it made me cry, too. It brought it all back to me, how *my* mum might have cried and been on television, begging someone not to hurt me.

In the newspaper it said how the Gardiners were a "devoted family". Gayle and her mum and dad got on really well and never had rows, and Gayle had been looking forward to helping them celebrate their twenty-fifth wedding anniversary. They'd been going to have a big family gathering, but now it was probably going to be cancelled.

Our head teacher was interviewed and said how Gayle was a good student, popular with her classmates and not in any kind of trouble. Reporters had talked to Ruby, who'd told them how she and Gayle had had this massive row because Gayle thought Ruby had been going out behind her back with her boyfriend.

"But it wasn't true," sobbed Ruby.

The paper went and interviewed the boyfriend anyway and discovered that he'd actually been at another club on Saturday night, with a totally different girl, so that put paid to my romantic notion that maybe Gayle had eloped.

I still clung to the one shred of hope, which was something I'd once read somewhere, that by far the majority of young people who go missing have run off for reasons of their own. Like maybe they're deep into drugs and no one knows about it, or they've got a secret boyfriend, or they don't like their new stepdad, or – well, just anything, really. In other words, simply because someone has disappeared doesn't necessarily mean they've been abducted. This was what I kept telling myself, but I wasn't convinced. And all the feelings I had experienced after my close shave with Paul came flooding back.

Gayle's sister, Ellie, was in our class. She didn't come to school for the first couple of days, and then when she came back almost nobody was brave enough to talk to her. We didn't know what to say. We all felt really sorry for her and desperately wanted to show it, but we were scared in case we upset her and set her off crying. Her face was already white and pinched, and sodden with tears.

Her best friend, Tasha, kept giving us these reproachful glares, like she thought we were cold and heartless and didn't care; but the one time Chloe went bouncing up, full of good intentions, she snarled at her to "Just go away! Ellie doesn't want to be *bothered*." It didn't exactly encourage the rest of us. Even Chloe, who as a rule is quite impervious to snubs, didn't go back for a second helping.

Every day we listened to the news, hoping that the police would have uncovered some clues, but nobody had come forward and they seemed as baffled as ever.

"Couldn't your mum help them?" said Dee. She said she'd once seen a film where a medium had been given something to hold that had belong to a girl who had disappeared, and the medium had "gone into a trance" and been able to tell the police that they would find the girl "buried in some woods by the side of a stream."

"And was she?" said Chloe.

Dee said she couldn't remember.

"Well, that was a lot of help," I said.

"Yes, but mediums *are* sometimes called in by the police," said Dee. "If we got something that belonged to Gayle and gave it to your mum—"

"Mum doesn't work that way," I said. "She has to have the person there, in front of her."

"*You* don't," said Chloe.

"Why don't we try it," urged Dee.

"Look, if Mum thought she could be of help, she'd go to the police herself," I said. "But she doesn't do that sort of thing."

"So what, exactly *does* she do?" said Chloe.

I explained that Mum tuned in to people's emotions. "Their hopes and fear. Dreams. Ambitions. Sort of... more psychological, I suppose."

I could tell from their silence that Dee and Chloe weren't too impressed.

"She really does help people get themselves sorted," I said. "She just doesn't do police-type stuff."

*

By Friday, it was almost a week since Gayle had disappeared. Still no one had come forward. The police had announced that they were going to stage a reconstruction on Saturday night, in the hope of jogging someone's memory. Dee and Chloe were coming to my place on Saturday for a sleepover. Last time we had gone to Chloe's, and next time would be at Dee's, which I was dreading as I didn't know how I would feel, sleeping under the same roof as her brother. I wasn't sure that I would be able to face it, and was already thinking up excuses why I couldn't go.

We sat upstairs in my bedroom that evening (Mum was in her consulting room with a client), wondering how the police reconstruction was going.

"There's got to be *someone* who remembers seeing her," I said. "I mean, how could you not notice someone like Gayle? She looks like a model!"

"Oh, do let's stop talking about it," begged Chloe. "It makes me feel all creepy. Let's play The Game!"

"We played it last time," I said.

"I know, but it'll take your mind off things." Chloe shot a glance at Dee. "What d'you reckon?"

"Yes, let's play it," said Dee. "It's better than just sitting here being morbid."

"But there's no point doing you two again," I said. "And I can't do anyone else 'cos you haven't brought anything."

"*I* have." Chloe plunged a hand into her bag and emerged triumphant with a gold locket on a chain. She dangled it before me. "See?"

"Who's it belong to?" I said.

"It's this girl my cousin knows. She's always asking me if you'll do her."

"We might as well," said Dee. "Otherwise we'll just spend all night glooming."

Between them, in the end, they talked me round. I was quite reluctant, and couldn't think why; but I took the locket and sat back on my heels on the bedroom floor while Dee and Chloe crouched on either side of me; Chloe cross-legged, Dee hugging her knees to her chest, waiting expectantly for me to perform.

I closed my eyes, letting the chain slip through my fingers. Concentrating. Focusing. Directing my energies. Something was there. Something...

Out of the ordinary. Something...

Powerful. Something—

And then it hit me. *Fear*. Wave upon wave of it. Cold, and gut-churning, drenching me in sweat; and somewhere a voice that screamed out in the darkness. *Help me! Help me!* But what could I do? Fear became panic. My mind thrashed in a frenzy, trying to find a way out, to break the connection.

"Jo? *Jo?*" Someone was shaking me. I dropped the chain and covered my face with my hands. I was trembling all over, and couldn't seem to stop.

"Jo!" Dee squatted in front of me, her face scrunched in concern. "What is it? What happened?"

"I – don't know. Who is this person?" I turned angrily, on Chloe. "Where does she come from? What do you know about her?"

 Chloe darted an anxious look at Dee.

"What's going on?" I cried. "What have you done?"

"It's my fault as much as Chloe's," said Dee.

"What is? What are you talking about? *Whose is it?*" I picked up the locket and hurled it as hard as I could across the room. "*Where did you get it from?*"

Then they told me. They confessed what they had done. They had gone to Ruby Simpson and asked her if she could lend them something that belonged to Gayle.

"We thought perhaps a... a book, or something. You know?"

A book might not have had so strong an impact; but Ruby had handed over the locket. It seemed she had borrowed it from Gayle the night they'd set out to go clubbing.

"What did you get from it?" whispered Dee.

I said, "Nothing. I don't know! I don't want to talk about it."

Chloe leaned in, closer. "Was it something scary?"

"*I don't want to talk about it!* You promised you'd never cheat me. You don't know what you're meddling with! I'm not ready for this sort of thing."

Dee looked downcast and said that she was sorry. Chloe muttered that they'd "just wanted to do something to help Gayle".

"Well, I can't help her!" I said. "What can I do? *I* don't know where she is!"

"But you think she's... in some sort of danger?" said Chloe.

That girl just never gives up.

"I think she's in trouble," I said. But everyone already knew that.

Dee picked up the locket and put it in her bag. "What shall we tell Ruby?"

"Just tell her I didn't see anything."

"But you did," said Chloe.

"I did not!" I snapped. "I *felt* things."

"So why don't we—"

"Oh, Chloe! Do shut up," said Dee. "Let's play some music and just forget about it."

We played some music, but I don't think any of us could forget. Certainly not me. I'd said that I hadn't seen anything, but it wasn't quite true. At the very moment that Dee had shaken me, and the link had been broken, I had had this sudden flash of being in someone else's body. Seeing through someone else's eyes. What I had seen was a car. I was in the car. And the car was familiar. I knew that I had been in it before – or one very like it. It was a Ka. A Ford Ka. A blue one...

What I couldn't work out, because I didn't have the experience, was whether I was really seeing through someone else's eyes – Gayle's eyes – or whether the waves of terror that had engulfed me had reactivated *my* terror and transported me back to that dreadful night, trapped in the car as we hammered towards the gravel pits.

There just seemed no way of knowing.

seven

THAT NIGHT THE dreams came back. I kept waking, shivering and terrified; scared of going to sleep again. It was a comfort knowing that Dee and Chloe were there with me, curled up on the floor in their sleeping bags, yet at the same time I was just so angry with them for deceiving me. I knew they had acted from the best of motives, but they had no idea of the damage they could do, getting me to play around with forces that I hadn't yet learnt to control.

I guess part of the reason I was so angry was that I knew, deep down, it was more my fault than theirs. I should never have agreed to play The Game in the first place; Mum had warned me against it often enough. Dee and Chloe weren't to know. To them it was just a fun way of passing the time. On this occasion it had been more serious because they had genuinely wanted to help Gayle. But why put it all on to me? What was I supposed to do? I didn't know where she was!

Next morning I took Mum her breakfast in bed, so that the three of us could pig out by ourselves in the kitchen. We turned on the radio to hear if there was any news, but all they said was that the police had staged their reconstruction. They didn't mention if anyone had come forward.

"Maybe it's a bit too soon," I said.

"Or maybe they wouldn't announce it till they'd checked it out," suggested Dee.

We agreed that the police probably didn't pass on everything they knew.

"Stands to reason," said Chloe. "They'd have to keep something back... clues, and stuff."

Dee had to leave early as she was going off to visit her grandparents. Her mum and dad were supposed to stop by and pick her up on their way, but when I went to answer the door I found Paul standing there. My heart went clunking right down into the pit of my stomach. Why did it always have to be him? Why was *he* always the one who turned up? It was like he was doing it on purpose to taunt me.

"Hi," he said; and he smiled. "Is Dee ready?"

I said, "I'll get her!" and slammed the door in his face and went galloping back down the hall. "Dee! It's your brother!"

"Paul?" Her face lit up. "Oh, good! I didn't think he was coming."

She sounded really happy; she obviously adored him. It was just another reason why I couldn't say anything. I told myself that of course I *would*, if I were really sure. Even if it meant a furious lecture from Mum, I wouldn't hesitate. But how could I know, for certain? Dee was one of my two best friends! I would have hated to do anything to hurt her.

We watched as she drove off, sitting with Paul in the back of her parents' Volvo. I wondered if Paul still had his little blue Ka, or if he had got rid of it. "Disposing of the evidence," I thought.

"He's really nice, isn't he?" said Chloe, as we went back indoors. "Paul... he's so lovely!"

I muttered, "He's OK."

"Don't you like him?"

"He's creepy," I said.

"Mm..." Chloe crinkled her nose as she considered it. "I sort of see what you mean. He's kind of, like... *quiet*."

I said, "Creepy. Why does he keep smiling all the time?"

"Does he?"

"Yes." I stretched my lips. "He's always doing it."

Chloe said she hadn't noticed. "P'raps he's just being friendly."

"He doesn't have to keep doing it. It just looks stupid, keeping on doing it. And why's he still living at home? Why isn't he married?"

"Not everyone gets married," said Chloe. "He could be gay."

"More like *weird*."

"Dee practically worships him," said Chloe.

"Yes, and that's another thing." I closed the kitchen door, in case our voices carried up the stairwell (remembering Mum's phenomenal, lynxlike hearing).

"He wasn't there when we first knew Dee. She never even mentioned him. We never even knew she *had* a brother. He just suddenly, like, appeared one day out of nowhere."

"Actually..." Chloe hesitated.

"Actually what?" I said.

"Actually, I shouldn't be telling you this 'cos I'm not really supposed to know, but I heard he'd been in hospital."

"What, like you mean he's been ill?"

"Sort of," said Chloe.

"What d'you mean, *sort of*?"

"He's been in Arlington Park," said Chloe.

For the second time that morning my heart went into free fall. Arlington Park is a psychiatric hospital. People only go there if they're too sick to be let out into the community. I stared at Chloe. Her face had turned bright scarlet, so I guessed it was something she'd been sworn not to tell.

"Is that really true?" I said. Chloe nodded. "It's not just you, making it up?"

"I don't make things up!"

She does; all the time. But she said she'd actually been there when her mum was discussing it with a friend of hers who cleaned for Dee's mum. (Imagine having someone to do your cleaning for you! But Dee's mum is a solicitor, so I suppose she can afford it.)

"Mum didn't let me listen any more," said Chloe, "she sent me away, and afterwards she told me I wasn't to go gossiping about it to anyone. I'm only telling *you*," she said, "'cos we're friends."

I swallowed. "So... what was... wrong with him?"

"Dunno. Didn't get that far," said Chloe. "But you have to be pretty bad to be locked up!"

We agreed that you did; and that that was almost certainly why Dee had never mentioned to us that she had a brother.

"I mean, you wouldn't want to talk about it, would you?" said Chloe. "So we mustn't ever let on that we know."

"I wouldn't," I said. The last thing I wanted was to talk to Dee about her brother.

"He's obviously all right," said Chloe, "or they wouldn't have let him out. But it's probably why he sometimes seems a bit strange."

"Let's not discuss it," I said.

"No," said Chloe, "we probably shouldn't. Not behind Dee's back."

"Not any time," I said.

Later on, I listened to the news again, with Mum.

"Still nothing," I said.

Mum shook her head.

"You'd think *someone* would have seen her!"

"People don't always want to get involved," said Mum.

"You mean they wouldn't go to the police even if they had seen something? That is just so antisocial!" I said.

"I'm afraid people often are," said Mum.

"But why?"

"Oh, Jo! For all sorts of reasons."

I frowned, trying to think of some. "You mean, like... if someone mightn't want the police to know they were there? Like if they were committing a robbery, or something?"

"That could be one reason," agreed Mum.

"Even if someone's life was at stake?"

I just couldn't believe anybody would stay silent. Mum said, well, maybe they wouldn't.

"There's still time. Let's just hope someone's memory's been jogged."

"When would we know?" I said. "When would they tell us?"

"That's up to them," said Mum. And then she looked across at my plate and said, "What a mess you're making!"

136

We were sitting in the kitchen, having Sunday lunch, and I'd been slowly churning my cauliflower cheese into some kind of sculpture.

"Actually, I don't really want it," I said. "I'm not very hungry."

"Try," urged Mum. "I'm aware it's easier said than done, but honestly, sweetheart, worrying isn't going to help."

"No, I know." I heaved a sigh, and did a bit more sculpting. "You know those Ka things?" I said.

"What car things?" said Mum.

"*Ka*. K-A. Ka."

"Oh, those! Yes. What about them? Did you fancy one?"

"No," I said. "I think they're horrible."

"Cheap to run."

"Yes, but they're horrible."

"So why did you mention them?"

"I was just wondering whether... they were popular."

"I should think so. You see quite a lot of them about."

"Do you?" I said.

"Well, I do," said Mum. "Why, anyway?"

"Oh, it's a – a project we're doing," I said. "Environmental studies."

"Yes, well, I should think they're probably a good thing," said Mum.

Depends who's driving them, I thought; and I forced down the mashed remains of my cauli cheese.

"I might like to do environmental work some day," I said.

"Well, that would be a good thing, too," said Mum. "Certainly an easier way of earning a living than delving into the depths of other people's minds,"

"Do you ever have bad experiences?" I said. "Do you ever... see things that are... frightening?"

"Occasionally."

"*Really* frightening?"

"Like what?" said Mum.

"Well, like... like if someone had done something evil, like... murdered someone, or something."

"No," said Mum. "I've never had that."

"What would you do? If you thought someone had murdered someone?"

"Oh, Jo, what a question! It's never arisen, so I've never really given much thought to it. In any case, how would I know whether it was real, or just a fantasy?"

138

"Couldn't you tell?" I said.

"Not necessarily. People have the oddest things going on inside their heads. I think probably, unless the circumstances were quite exceptional, I would just have to... take no account of it."

I was so relieved when Mum said that. How would you know whether it was real or a fantasy? Not even Mum could be certain!

"What is all this, anyway?" she said. "Another project?"

"It's for a story," I said.

"A horror story?"

"Well – yes." I gave a little giggle, which even to my ears sounded somewhat hysterical.

"Wouldn't it be better just to write something about everyday life?" said Mum.

I thought, this *is* about everyday life; but to keep Mum happy, and set her mind at rest, I said that she was probably right.

"I'll try and think of something else."

But I couldn't. I was obsessed by thoughts of Gayle. Where she might be, what might be happening to her. All the stories I'd ever read about young girls being abducted came crowding and jostling into my mind. Had any of them ever had a happy ending? *Ever?* Had anyone ever been found alive?

It was like a nightmare, ongoing, without end. And I kept thinking, if it was like a nightmare for me, what must it be like for Gayle's mum and dad, and Ellie?

Monday morning, we heard on the news that two women had come forward as a result of the reconstruction. They said that they had seen Gayle talking to a man in a car, on the ground floor level of the car park.

They didn't know whether she had just got out of the car, or whether she was just about to get into the car, or whether she was just having a chat before going on her way. They were only passing through, and hadn't waited to find out.

"Why didn't they come forward earlier?" I cried. "If they're so sure it was Gayle?"

Mum said the whole point of a reconstruction was that it would jolt people into remembering things they might otherwise have forgotten, or not even realised they had seen.

"Doesn't seem to have jolted very many of them," I said, glumly.

At school, everybody was talking about "the latest development" (as they said on the news); but quietly, almost furtively, in corners or behind desk lids.

"Don't really see that it's going to be much help," I said, as I walked round the field with Dee and Chloe at first break. "I mean, they don't know whether she actually got *into* the car... they don't even know what sort of car it *was*."

"It says in the paper," said Chloe. "Least, it did in my mum's."

Chloe's mum read the *Daily Mail*, so later on, when I had a free period and was meant to be doing homework, I went to the library and had a look. It didn't actually say very much more. Neither of the women could remember anything about the car except that it been blue, and "small". Like a Mini, or a Micra, or a Ford Fiesta.

Or a Ka.

eight

I PROBABLY SHOULDN'T have blurted everything out to
Chloe. Chloe, of all people! I knew how scatty she was.
Chloe has loads of good points – she is bright, she is
bubbly, she is a whole lot of fun. But she is such a
blabbermouth. Just because you are best friends with
someone doesn't mean that you are blind to their faults;
experience should have told me that confiding in Chloe
was not the wisest thing I had ever done. But I was in a
panic! I had found it difficult to believe when Mum had

told me how people "don't always want to get involved", how they wouldn't necessarily go to the police even if they had seen something. How could they *not*? How could they possibly stay silent when a girl's life was at stake? Now here I was, doing that very thing. Going to school, chatting to friends, moaning about double maths, grumbling about too much homework, when all the time I had information that could be important. I knew that I had to tell someone. So I told Chloe.

We were sitting on the terrace together at lunch time, in the usual howling gale which blows across from the playing field. Dee wasn't with us, she was at a meeting. Dee was always going off to meetings; she is a very public-spirited kind of person. If she had been there, I don't know what I would have done. Waited till I got home, perhaps. I would certainly never have said anything in front of Dee. But Chloe was giggling at the way I'd behaved in maths when Mr McFarlane, in his sarcastic way, had asked me if I intended "touching down on this planet any time soon" and I had stared at him, goggle-eyed, and said, "In a right-angled triangle?" which is somewhat, if not indeed totally, meaningless, but was all I could dredge up on the spur of the moment.

"I didn't hear him," I said to Chloe. "I didn't hear what he said!"

"In a right-angled triangle! It wasn't even geometry," gurgled Chloe.

Ha ha, hugely ha. I could see that it was probably quite amusing to small minds, and I would probably have laughed like a drain myself if it had happened to anyone else, but I thought it was quite uncalled for to suggest, as Mr McFarlane witheringly did, that my mind was "cluttered up with cheesy images of the opposite sex". He had some nerve! What did he know about my mind? Needless to say, Mel Sanders had slewed round in her desk to look at me and contorted her features into prunelike disapproval.

"Naughty naughty!"

I'd felt like slapping her. I'd also felt like jumping up and rushing out of the room. My mind was in a torment – and *not* with cheesy thoughts of the opposite sex. Mr McFarlane and his stupid irritating maths was way down the scale of anything which might merit attention.

"I suppose you were thinking about *him*?" said Chloe. "Dreamboat Danny! *Swoon*."

"Actually," I said, "I was thinking about Gayle."

"Oh. Well! Yes." Chloe pulled a face. "I keep thinking about her, too. It must be so awful for poor Ellie!"

"And her mum and dad. Not *knowing*. That must be the most terrible part!"

Chloe agreed that it must. But surely, she said, Gayle wouldn't have gone off with a total stranger? I said that she might, if she'd just had a row with Ruby.

"You really think so?" said Chloe.

"I don't know! I don't know! But things happen – people do these things! You know what those women said about the car? A small blue car? You know they said they didn't know what make it was but it could have been a Ka – K-A, Ka! You know! Those little ones?"

"Y-yes." Chloe was eyeing me, uncertainly. I suppose I did sound slightly mad. It just suddenly all came spurting out of me.

"Well…" I took a breath. "I got into one of those."

"You mean, like… with a stranger?"

"Someone I didn't properly know."

Chloe chewed at her lower lip. She obviously sensed that this was something serious because for once she managed not to say anything; just waited, in silence, for me to continue.

"It was Paul."

"*Dee's* Paul?"

I nodded. "That night at the Pizza Palace… he gave me a lift."

"I remember! Dee was cross 'cos you'd jumped out of the car. You said – *oh*." Chloe clapped a hand to her mouth. "He didn't—"

"No. But he drove me the wrong way, he took me down Gravelpit Hill, it was really, really scary. And now there's all this about Gayle, and a blue car, and… you know on Saturday, we played The Game?"

"Yes," said Chloe, "and you went all peculiar."

147

"I didn't go peculiar, I saw something... I was in a car. It was a car I'd been in before. Or a car *like* one I'd been in before. Only I couldn't work out whether it was me, or whether it was Gayle, so that's why I didn't say anything, 'cos you can't always tell the difference. But now there's these women, and a blue car, and *I don't know what to do!*"

My voice came out in a self-pitying wail. Some Year 9 girls gave me these weird looks as they walked past.

"What do I do?" I said. "I don't know what to do!"

"There's only one thing you can do," said Chloe. "Go to the police. Jo, you've got to!"

"But suppose it wasn't really Gayle? Suppose it was just *me*?"

"It's the same car," said Chloe.

"It *might* be the same car."

"It's the same colour. And he did try to abduct you! I don't know why you didn't say something before!"

"I didn't want Mum knowing about it. And I didn't want to upset Dee. I still don't want to!"

"But if he's done something to Gayle, and he did something to you, he could do something to Dee, as well. She could be in danger!"

"Except he didn't actually *do* anything to me."

"No, 'cos you managed to escape! Think how you'd

148

feel," said Chloe, "if something happened to Dee and you could have stopped it."

She didn't say, think how you'll feel if something's happened to Gayle, but she didn't have to, because I was already feeling it. I knew that I should have gone to the police ages ago, or at least told Mum.

"Jo, you've got to report it," said Chloe. "I think you should go and see Miss Adams."

"She'll be so angry," I quavered.

Miss Adams is our head teacher, and is quite frightening at the best of times. But I couldn't really argue; Chloe was only telling me what I already knew.

"I'll come with you," she said. "I'll give you moral support."

She marched me back into school and along to the office, where she announced in ringing tones for everyone within a five mile radius to hear, that "Jo has to see Miss Adams. It's urgent!" Mrs Biswas, the school secretary, raised an eyebrow. She is probably not used to Year 8 pupils demanding to see the Head. It's usually the other way round, the Head demanding to see you. I was trembling now. I was probably looking like

I was in a bit of a state, because Mrs Biswas asked me quite gently, and not in her normal dragon tones, what the problem was. Chloe, all self-important, said, "She's got something to tell her. About Gayle."

Well, that was it; Mrs Biswas immediately went into action. Within seconds – it seemed like only seconds – I was in Miss Adams's room pouring out my story (Chloe having been sent packing, much to her indignation). Miss Adams listened to me in

grave silence, and at the end she said, "Is your mother at home?" Oh, God, she was going to ring Mum! But Mum would have had to hear sooner or later, so it was probably just as well.

While we were waiting for Mum to arrive, Miss Adams asked me lots of questions, which I did my best to answer truthfully and in as much detail as possible; then when Mum appeared, looking worried and flustered, and obviously wondering what kind of ghastly trouble I had got myself into, we had to go through it all again for her benefit, only this time, thank goodness, Miss Adams did most of the talking. Every now and again she would say, "Is that right, Joanne? Is that what happened?" and I would mutter "Yes" and do my best not to catch Mum's eye.

Neither of them lectured me, or told me how criminally stupid I'd been. The lectures came later. And how! But that day, in Miss Adams's study, they were mainly concerned about Gayle. Miss Adams rang the police, and two CID people came round, like, at the double. So then it all had to be told for the third time, and the more I heard it the more guilty I felt at having kept quiet for so long.

Nobody actually blamed me for not saying anything, though one of the CID officers, the female one, did ask me why I hadn't. I went scarlet and mumbled that I hadn't wanted to upset Dee. Mum looked at me rather hard, as if she knew that that was only part of the reason. Her look seemed to say, "I'll speak to you later, my girl." (Which she did, but I think I will draw a veil over that.)

After I had been thoroughly grilled – I believe that is the correct word for when someone is being questioned by the police – Mum and I had to go down to the police station. In a police car! (They brought us back later to pick up our own car.)

I felt very self-conscious, walking out of school with two CID people. Even though they were in plain clothes I felt that everyone who saw them would guess they were police, and would wonder what I had done. As it happened, it was the middle of the first period after lunch, so lessons were in progress and I don't think anybody did see me, but I still didn't like it. I felt like I had committed some crime and was under arrest. Mum was grim the whole time, and I knew she was saving up things to say to me.

Once at the police station I was taken to an interview room, where I had to give a statement. It should have been easy, because by now I had told the story at least three times, but I kept worrying that I wasn't remembering properly, or wasn't saying it right. Like when the police wanted to know – *again*, 'cos they had already asked me once – whether Paul had done anything to me, and I said he hadn't; but then I suddenly remembered how he had leaned across me to get to the glove compartment and how there had been a screwdriver in there, and I had screamed and jerked away, and he had almost lost control of the wheel. That was something I hadn't said first time round, because it didn't really count as "doing anything", and it had

somehow just slipped my memory. But as soon as I said it, they pounced, and wanted to know more, like did I think he was actually reaching for the screwdriver; to which I had to say that I didn't know. All I knew was that he had driven me down Gravelpit Hill and I had been terrified.

There was one thing I didn't tell the police and hadn't told Miss Adams, either. I didn't say anything about my session with Dee and Chloe, when they had given me Gayle's chain to hold. I didn't think that they would understand; and, besides, it didn't really seem relevant. But I did tell Mum about it, when we finally arrived back home. I'm not sure what prompted me, except perhaps that I needed to get it off my chest. And oh, it was such a relief! I realised that I had felt really guilty about it.

I thought Mum would be angry, but she said that what concerned her far more was that I had accepted a lift from a virtual stranger, rather than that I had "misused my gift".

"I know the temptation. Believe me, I do!"

"Did *you* ever misuse your gift?" I said.

Mum said she was ashamed to admit that she did. Mum had grown up in ignorance of the fact that she had psychic powers. Her gran – my great gran, that I never knew – had been reputed to "see things", and her mum – my gran – had once predicted that her next door neighbour would find her missing wedding ring "down the side of the sofa", and she had.

"But everyone just put that down to a lucky guess."

Nobody ever warned Mum about misusing her gift, because nobody ever realised that she had it. Mum herself only knew that sometimes, when she was with someone, she would get these "feelings". One day at school she borrowed a pen from her best friend, Liz, and she got really strong feelings.

"Of excitement," said Mum. "So I asked Liz and she said it was true, she *was* excited. She was going up to London, to the ballet. So then I started doing it deliberately... borrowing things from people. Pens, rubbers, rulers, seeing what feelings they gave me. It was just a game – except in the end it wasn't, as you've discovered."

I asked Mum what had happened, and she said that even after all these years she didn't really like to talk about it.

"Which is why I've never told you before. It still makes me feel bad. I borrowed something from a girl called Janice Baker. She was one of those girls... we all used to gang up on her. I suppose today you'd call her a nerd, or a wimp. We just thought she was wet.

Anyway, I had these really dark feelings come over me, like someone was walking across my grave. A few days later we learnt that she'd been taken to hospital... she'd been in a car crash."

"Did she die?" I said.

"Yes." Mum nodded. "I know it wasn't anything I did, and there was probably nothing I could have done to stop it, but after that I didn't play the game any more."

"I'm not going to play it, either!" I said.

"Well, I'm glad about that," said Mum. "But, Jo, I'm really horrified that at your age, after all the times we've talked about it, you could be so foolish as to get into a car with someone you don't know. How could you do such a thing? What were you thinking of? No! Don't tell me." She held up a hand. "I remember... what was it? Glitter boots! All for a pair of tacky fashion items that wouldn't last five minutes, you go and put your life in jeopardy! I'm at a loss. It hardly bears thinking about!"

She went on this vein for quite some time. This is the part I'm drawing a veil over, as it was rather uncomfortable. I didn't try defending myself because I knew that I couldn't.

"All I can say," said Mum, "is that I hope to goodness you've learnt your lesson."

I said, "Mum, I have!"

"Even I," said Mum, "have never done anything quite as stupid as that. And heaven knows," she said, "I've done some stupid things in my time!"

"It's just that he was Dee's brother," I pleaded.

"I hear you," said Mum. "But has it never occurred to you that people are always someone's brother? Someone's father? Someone's husband?"

I hung my head.

"Anyway," she said, "you did the right thing in the end. It's a pity you didn't do it sooner, but—"

"Dee's going to hate me!" I said.

"It won't be easy," agreed Mum, "for either of you. But she's a sensible girl, I'm sure she'll understand. She couldn't expect you to keep quiet indefinitely. You had to speak out, Jo. I know Dee's your friend, but if there's any danger at all of him doing to other girls what he might have done to you... even Dee herself could be at risk."

"I know." I heaved a sigh. "That's what Chloe said."

"Well, Chloe talked sense for once."

"But suppose Paul isn't anything to do with it?" I said.

"In that case, there's no harm done. At least the police will be able to eliminate him from their enquiries. Even so," said Mum, "we still have to ask ourselves why he was taking you down Gravelpit Hill."

"He said he liked it better than the other way."

"Even though the other way is half again as short?"

"Yes, and why did he have a screwdriver?" I said.

Mum said she wasn't so bothered about that. "People might have a screwdriver for all sorts of legitimate reasons. But to take you off in the wrong direction... that needs some explaining."

A few minutes after I'd had this conversation with Mum, the phone rang. It was Dee.

"Where were you?" she demanded. "What happened?"

I said, "I—"

"What?"

"I had to—"

"*What?*"

"Had to—"

"Chloe said something about you going to see Miss Adams."

"Yes," I said. "I had to go and see Miss Adams."

"About Gayle?"

"Yes. I had to – had to – tell her something."

"What?"

"I c-can't s-say, it's..."

"Does Chloe know?"

"Ch-Chloe?" I said.

"She's got that look. You know that look she gets? When she's hiding something?"

I swallowed.

"If you could tell her, I should have thought you could've told me," said Dee.

She was obviously feeling hurt. I could understand it; I would have felt hurt in her place. How could I tell Chloe something and not tell Dee? I muttered that I had told Chloe before I had been warned by Miss Adams "not to go talking about it".

"You weren't there," I said. "You'd gone off somewhere."

"I was at a meeting," said Dee.

"Yes. Well... this is what I'm saying. You weren't there! If you had have b—"

"Hang on," said Dee. "Something's happening. I'll ring you back."

As I put the phone down, I found my hand was shaking. What did she mean, something was happening? Was it the police? Had they gone round there? I had these visions of Paul, being dragged from the house in

handcuffs. Except that surely they wouldn't do that until they knew for certain? Surely they would just ask him – politely – to accompany them to the police station for questioning. That was what they did. They didn't go round arresting people before they had proof. Did they?

Before I could consult Mum, the phone had rung again. This time it was Chloe, in a state of barely suppressed excitement.

"Hi! What happened? Did you go to the police?"

I said, "I don't want to talk about it. Dee's just rung me. It was awful!"

I heard a little gasp from Chloe's end. "Does she know? Have they taken him away?"

I said, "*I don't know.* We shouldn't be talking about it!"

"I didn't tell her anything," said Chloe, virtuously.

"You told her I'd gone to Miss Adams about Gayle!"

"Oh. Yes – well. I had to tell her *something*."

I didn't see why she had to, but I wasn't about to get into an argument.

"Look, I have to go," I said. "Tea's ready, and I'm expecting Dee to ring back."

"OK." Chloe said it quite amiably. She's always very good-natured, which is just as well since she spends a large part of her life putting her foot in things, upsetting people and being yelled at. *Chloe, for goodness' sake! Chloe, you IDIOT! Chloe, how COULD you?* She never takes offence.

"See you tomorrow," she said.

"Yeah," I said. "See you."

I spent the rest of the evening waiting in a kind of dread for Dee to ring back, but she never did; and on the news next morning they announced that there had been "fresh developments in the case of missing teenager Gayle Gardiner".

A local man was helping police with their inquiries.

nine

IT HAD NEVER occurred to me to swear Chloe to secrecy; I mean, I just never thought. I knew she was a blabbermouth, I knew the only way you could rely on her to keep a secret was if you sealed her lips with sticky tape and tied her hands behind her back. But this was more than just a secret. It was more than just our usual girly chitchat about who was going out with whom and who had stolen someone else's boy friend. It was something I had told her in strictest confidence. I never for one moment imagined she would go and blurt it out – and especially not to Gayle's sister.

I could sense the minute I walked into the classroom that the atmosphere was tense. Ellie was huddled in a corner with two of her friends; she was crying, and they both had their arms round her. Other people were standing around in little groups, looking shocked and not talking. I saw Dee, sitting at her desk, with her head bent over a book; and Chloe, hovering on the fringe of Ellie and her friends.

I was about to go over to Dee when Mr McFarlane breezed in, brisk and ill-tempered as usual, to start on the first lesson of the day. Maths, heaven help us! Dee, being some kind of genius, was in the A group for maths, which meant she took herself off to a different classroom and thus I didn't get a chance to speak to her; for which, to be honest, I was profoundly grateful. I just didn't know what I would find to say. Or if she would even let me.

After maths we had French. Dee and I were in the same group for French and normally sat next to each other, but that morning Dee deliberately chose a desk as far away from me as it was possible to get. As far away from everyone else, as well. I could understand why *I* was being shunned – if I had had a brother and my best friend had shopped him to the police, I probably wouldn't want to talk to them, either; but what had the others done to upset her?

Shayna Phillips, who was sitting near me, leant across to whisper.

"It must be so awful for her!"

I said, "W-what must?"

"Well – you know! Her brother."

I obviously looked confused. Which I was.

"Being arrested," mouthed Shayna.

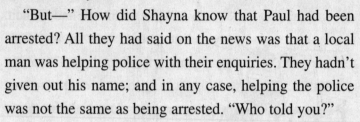

"But—" How did Shayna know that Paul had been arrested? All they had said on the news was that a local man was helping police with their enquiries. They hadn't given out his name; and in any case, helping the police was not the same as being arrested. "Who told you?"

Mrs Armstrong came in at that point. Shayna had just the time to whisper the one word, "Chloe."

"*Chloe?*" I couldn't believe it. I just couldn't believe that even Chloe could be that... untrustworthy. That *disloyal*. How could she do such a thing?

"She told Ellie."

I opened my mouth to say, "*Ellie?*" but Mrs Armstrong got in ahead of me.

"Joanne, I cannot believe that my somewhat ample presence has escaped your attention?"

Mrs Armstrong is rather plump, hence her reference to ample presence, which would normally have made everyone laugh. Today people just gave nervous smiles. I gazed across at Dee, willing her to look in my direction, but she kept her head down the whole lesson. I felt so bad! She must have thought that Chloe and I had ganged up on her, gone behind her back – which of course, in a way, we had. I wished with all my heart that I had never confided in Chloe. Dee would probably still have hated me, for going to the police, but at least no one else would have known about it. Now, thanks to Chloe – thanks to me – it seemed that the entire school knew. Certainly everybody in our class.

"But I only told Ellie!" wailed Chloe, when we met up at break.

"You shouldn't have told *anyone*," I said.

"You didn't say not to!"

"I shouldn't have had to say not to. You should have known! How do you think Dee feels, everyone going round talking about her?"

"They're not talking about her, they're talking about her brother!"

"Oh, for goodness' *sake*." I think I actually stamped my foot. I was just so angry with her!

"Look, I'm sorry," said Chloe. "I'm sorry, I'm sorry! I can't say more than that, can I?"

"I don't know why you ever said anything to begin with!"

"I didn't mean to, it just kind of... slipped out. I was talking to Ellie."

"*So?*"

"So – I don't know! It just happened. So what? It's no big deal. It'll be in all the newspapers soon, anyway."

"Only if they actually arrest him, which they haven't done yet. Not as far as I know. Why did you have to go and say they'd *arrested* him?"

"'Cos I thought they had." Chloe said it sullenly. "I thought it was the same thing."

"Well, it's not! They're just talking to him. He's *helping* them. He could be innocent!"

"You said—"

"I said I'd got into his car and he'd driven me the wrong way."

"Well, there you are! Even if he didn't take Gayle, he tried to take you, so he's *not* innocent. What I don't understand," said Chloe, suddenly jumping on some grievance of her own, "is why you couldn't tell? When he offered you a lift... you're supposed to be psychic! Why couldn't you *tell*?"

I snapped, "It doesn't work that way!"

"Seems to me it doesn't work any way," muttered Chloe. "First you say you've seen him in a car with Gayle, then you say you're not sure, then—"

"Oh, shut up," I said, "and don't be stupid!"

Not very clever, I admit; but there were times when Chloe just got me *so livid.*

We didn't see Dee all during break, and she kept well away from us – and from everyone else – at lunch time, too. It wasn't till school let out at 3.30 that we came face to face. We arrived at the gates at the same moment, and couldn't really avoid each other. Before I could say anything, Dee had put her face up close to mine and hissed, "I'll never forgive you, Joanne Daley! Never, never, never, as long as I live!"

When I got home, I burst into tears. I hardly ever cry, I am just not a crying sort of person; but Dee was my best friend! My *very* best friend.

"She hates me!" I wept. "She's never going to forgive me!"

"Oh, Jo, I'm sure she will, in time," said Mum. "Don't forget, this must have come as a terrible shock to her."

"It's Chloe's fault," I said. "Going and telling everyone!"

"That certainly can't have helped," agreed Mum.

"But I was the one who went to the police! I'm the one she hates! I don't know how she found out it was me," I wailed. "Why did they have to tell her?"

Mum said they might have asked her questions, trying to see if I had ever mentioned anything to her.

"I wish I'd never mentioned it to anyone," I sobbed. "I wish I'd never gone to the police in the first place!"

"Jo, you had to," said Mum. "You know you had to. You did the right thing."

I may have done the right thing – but I had lost my best friend. I also had this feeling that Chloe and I wouldn't ever get back to being close again. We'd sort of made up after our breaktime spat, but without Dee to complete the threesome, things just weren't the same. We needed Dee to give us substance. Without her, our relationship was so flimsy I felt that sooner or later we were just going to float apart.

Chloe rang me that evening. Aggressively she said, "Look, I'm *sorry*. OK?"

"No," I shouted, "it's not OK! Think how Dee must be feeling."

"Pity you

didn't think of that before you went to the police," said Chloe.

We rang off in a huff, but then I thought about it, and I thought perhaps I'd been ungracious, because after all Chloe had said she was sorry, so after a bit I rang her back and said that *I* was sorry.

"I shouldn't have snapped at you."

"It's all right, it doesn't matter now," said Chloe. "They've found her! Gayle. She's alive! It's on the news, go and see."

I rushed off immediately to put the television on. I was just in time to hear that "The missing teenager, Gayle Gardiner, has been found by a man out walking his dog in Tanfield Woods, only a few miles away from where she was last seen before she disappeared, over a week ago."

At first when I heard it, my blood ran cold and I thought Chloe had got it wrong, because almost always when they

171

say "found by someone walking their dog" they mean that a body has been found. Also, it has to be said, Chloe is not the most reliable informant. She once told me that I had got "eighty-six per cent" for a maths exam. Un-be-lieve-able! But she swore that she had seen it.

"With my own eyes! It was there... Joanne Daley, eighty-six per cent."

Well, it turned out to be *twenty*-six, and ever since then I have always taken whatever she says with a large pinch of salt. So when I heard the words "a man walking his dog" my heart just went *thunk*, and for the first time in my life I thought I might actually be going to faint. I had to sink into a chair to stop myself from falling. I almost missed the bit that came next. Mum wasn't there (she was in her room, doing a consultation), so I snatched up the phone and rang Chloe back and shrieked, "What did they say, what did they say? Did they say she's all right?"

"Yes, she's in hospital. They think she was being held prisoner and managed to escape."

"Did anything, like – uh! You know. Happen to her?"

"Dunno," said Chloe. "They didn't say. They just said she'd been found."

"So they didn't say who'd taken her?"

"No, but if it's him," said Chloe, "she'll be able to tell them."

One part of me almost wanted it to be Paul, because then I could stop feeling guilty. If he'd really been holding Gayle against her will, not even Dee could blame me for going to the police. But there was another part of me which desperately *didn't* want it to be him, because I thought that it would break Dee's heart, and she was still my best friend even if she had stopped talking to me.

Next morning, I watched the news with Mum. By this time they had a few more details, which I think Mum would rather I hadn't heard, and perhaps I would rather not have heard, too, but you can't hide your head in the sand. These things happen, and it is no use going through life thinking that everything is wonderful, because lots of things just aren't. Lots of things are horrible and frightening and make you feel sick.

"I just thank heaven she managed to get away," said Mum. "Goodness only knows what the poor girl went through, but at any rate they'll be able to do DNA testing, and that will put paid to all the uncertainty."

She meant about Paul, of course. There was still this big question mark hanging over him.

"Don't worry," said Mum. "I'm sure it will be resolved very quickly."

In spite of not being at all convinced that I really wanted to know, I couldn't stop myself buying a newspaper on the way in to school and reading about what had happened to Gayle. How she had got into a car in the car park with someone she just knew vaguely, by sight. She had "seen him around" a few times, at clubs and discos; he was "sort of" familiar. Most probably (this was what I thought when I read it) she had been in a state after her big row with Ruby, because having a row with your best friend *does* get you into a state, and she just hadn't been thinking clearly.

There were some people who might say she had been stupid and old enough to know better, but I knew how easy it was, even when you have been warned over and over by your mum, by your teachers, by just about everybody.

All the time that I was reading about Gayle, I kept thinking how it could have been me. It could have been me who was abducted. It could have been me who was kept prisoner. It could have been me who was assaulted. I had been lucky: Gayle hadn't. Chloe seemed to think that she had. She pointed out that she had *got away*; but I remembered all the nightmares I had had after just nearly being abducted – or thinking that I was being abducted, because by now, after all this while, I felt that I could no longer be sure. Had Paul really been going to take me to the gravel pits? Or had I just imagined it? Chloe, when I told her my doubts, scoffed at the idea.

"Why did he take you down that road if he wasn't going to the gravel pits?"

"He might just have been going the long way round," I said.

"But *why*?" said Chloe. "What would be the point?"

I didn't have any answer to that. I just knew that the panic had stayed with me for weeks, and I couldn't help wondering how Gayle was going to cope.

Dee wasn't in school that morning, and neither was Ellie. Even if Dee had been, I probably wouldn't have found the courage to go and talk to her, however much I felt the need to unburden myself. To explain why I had done what I had done: to try and make her understand. In lots of ways, I am the most terrible coward. It would have shrivelled me completely if Dee had refused to listen; or worse yet, had told me that she hated me.

That evening, we heard that a twenty-three-year-old man was in police custody, charged with "the kidnapping of schoolgirl Gayle Gardiner".

It wasn't Paul.